Lust

for

Blood

Lust
for
Blood

Lauren Milfinger

C.E.B. Pubs
Dublin, Ohio

Lust for Blood

For information, please contact:
C.E.B. Pubs
editor@cebpubs.com
http://cebpubs.com

This book is a work of fiction. Names, character, places, and inci-dents are either the product of the author's imagination or are used fictitiously. Any resemblance to actual events, locales, businesses, or persons, living or dead, is entirely coincidental. Cover photo posed by a professional model, and nothing contained in this book is to be in any way construed as representative of the actual character or conduct of the model.

ISBN-16: 978-1-943288-14-4
ISBN-10: 1-943288-14-3

Published in the United States of America

For my darling
Joanna,
You naughty little girl

I: Lady Anna Corwin's Journal

Wednesday, 3rd July— So much has happened, and yet we have only just finished our late breakfast. Suzanne Willis, my good friend from school, has come to visit. She will be staying with us for three weeks, and it is so wonderful to be able to catch up on all that has passed since we were graduated and went out into the world.

To think, it has been all of three years since we left school. My birthday was last week, so now I'm an old woman of twenty-two years, whilst Suzanne is still but twenty-one, and will remain so for five more months.

I had been so looking forward to seeing her again. I was awake a few minutes past one o'clock this morning. Jackson had Thunderer hitched to the Victoria when I came out through the kitchen door, precisely at two o'clock. We had made this journey enough times to know how long it would take, but as this time the journey would be made in the middle of the night, we had allowed an extra half hour. Suzanne's train was scheduled to arrive at half three. Unless there was an unforeseen problem, we should be at the station twenty minutes before that. As Jackson kept the carriages in pristine condition, and Thunderer was a most reliable coach horse, I anticipated no problems.

Naturally, with a journey of several miles over dark country roads, both Jackson and I were prepared for emergencies. I had my little revolver in my bag, and Jackson would have his bulldog tucked away in a pocket. There had been no reports of highwaymen in this region for many years, yet we still took precautions.

We arrived at the station at 3:12, according to Jackson's watch. He stayed with the horse and carriage, whilst I walked through the waiting room and out onto the platform. There were several benches under the overhanging roof, and I seated myself on one of them.

An elderly couple was seated on one of the other benches. They had a large trunk and two big cases with them, so I presumed they would be boarding the train, and were not waiting for someone to get off.

The train puffed into the station two minutes behind schedule, according to the platform clock. The elderly couple, with the help of a porter, immediately set about getting their things loaded into the baggage waggon.

I hurried along the platform to where the first-class carriages had stopped. Only three compartment doors opened, and I saw Suzanne descend from the centre door, carrying a small bag. A porter, carrying two more, significantly larger bags, followed her as she hurried up the platform.

We embraced, in a properly subdued and decorous manner, with the usual quick pecks to the cheek, and I led Suzanne and the porter through the station to the waiting Victoria.

Jackson secured Suzanne's bags, then helped each of us up into the open coach. As we were settling into the seat, Jackson mounted the box seat, took the reins, and shook them to send Thunderer trotting away. We would be back to Muntglare about half four.

'This is so exciting,' Suzanne commented, when we were on our way.

'You must be exhausted,' I said. 'Travelling all that distance, and in the middle of the night, too.'

She shook her pretty head, smiling sweetly. 'Not at all,' she said. 'I was asleep for much of the journey. I imagine *you* are the one who will be in need of rest.'

'A few hours of sleep *would* do nicely,' I admitted.

'Well, dear Anna,' she said, 'while I'm not *too* tired, I suppose I could do with a bit more rest as well.' She frowned. 'Your brother won't think it improper, will he, if we sleep late this morning?'

I found myself laughing gaily. 'There is very little,' I said, that Edwin thinks is improper. 'As for sleeping late, well, he does that himself rather more often than not.'

'Wonderful. Is he a proper gentleman, dear Anna? Of course, I know he's an earl, but I've met more than a few earls who were right pigs if you gave them the slightest opportunity.'

'Fear not. Edwin is quite the most proper sort you'd ever wish to meet.'

'Yet there's little he thinks is improper? Now you confuse me.'

'I mean, dear, that he's a proper gentleman. You need have no fears for your virtue in his house." I leaned closer and lowered my voice. 'Unless you wish to indulge your sensuality, that is.'

'You mean, he would corrupt me, but only if I wished it?'

'Quite so.'

'I'm intrigued.'

We drove along in silence for a while. The carbide lamps threw their twin circles of light only a few feet in front of the carriage, so Jackson was urging Thunderer along in a slow trot. I've been told horses see better in the dark than people. I have no idea if this is true.

Suzanne was nodding off as we drove. I supposed her story of sleeping in the railway carriage was somewhat exaggerated. I had no idea whether she'd had the compartment to herself, or if there were others riding in it. If she were not alone, I suspect she might have dozed, but I doubt she'd allow herself to truly sleep.

She came to herself as the carriage turned from the dirt lane onto the brick-paved drive leading up to the New Lodge. One of the lights glared briefly across the old bronze plaque with the name of the estate, Muntglare.

'I have always wondered about that name,' Suzanne said. 'Where does it come from, "Muntglare?"'

'An English corruption of a much older French name, I fear,' I replied. 'I'm told it was originally "Mont Gloire," but that over many years it was changed to its current form. Parts of the old house date back to just after the Conquest.'

'Oh, how interesting. Will we be staying in that part of the house?'

'Not at all. The old house is unused to-day. We live in the New Lodge, which was built by my father in 1879, so, you see, it's all quite up to date. Even *we* are older than the house.'

'The house is only sixteen-years-old? I'm a little disappointed. I was expecting something ancient looking.'

The coach rattled into the kitchen yard. I don't believe Suzanne was *too* disappointed. While the New Lodge was, of course, quite literally still new, the architect had designed it to mimic a much older structure. It was built in the Romanesque style, designed by an American my father had imported, who seemed to have a flair for that sort of thing. A great pile of stone and brick, complete with rounded towers, leaded-glass windows, and a steeply pitched slate roof punctured by numerous small gables and dormers, only the bottom row of which could conveniently be seen through from the attic. Despite being new, and filled with all the latest conveniences, it managed to look quite ancient.

My personal maid, O'Leary, collected Suzanne's bags and took them up to my room. I had naturally decided to have her stay with me during her week here. We had shared a room a school. It seemed only natural to do the same whilst she was visiting. It would allow us to chatter and gossip as we fell asleep. It might, I hoped, allow for other things as well.

My room was dark as we followed O'Leary inside. I struck a match and lit the two gas sconces that flanked the door. O'Leary placed Suzanne's bags on a chest and set to work unpacking them and transferring the contents to the bottom two drawers of my tall chest.

'These dresses will need ironing, mum,' she commented. 'I'll take them now and have them looking lovely before breakfast.'

'That would be wonderful,' Suzanne replied.

While O'Leary was putting away Suzanne's things, I had lit the paraffin lamps on the small tables on either side of the bed. These were the latest, tubular wick, central draught lamps, which give quite a bright light if adjusted properly. I set them to burn quite low, so that there would be enough light in the room to see after the gas sconces were turned off, but not so much that the glare would keep us awake.

O'Leary had soon finished her duties, collected the wrinkled dresses, and departed. Being well trained, I knew she would not return until I rang for her after we awakened. I suppose one of the advantages of being a lady's maid is that she may sleep a bit later than the other servants, for her sole concern is my welfare.

'When I see the number of servants you have,' Suzanne said, 'I must admit I feel a bit envious. We have only a couple in our home, and they are rather elderly. I'm afraid my mother and I do more than our share of the domestic chores. But, of course, we are not nearly so wealthy as your family, living on the annuity my father established for us before he died. £350 a year is certainly adequate for two women, but it doesn't allow for a large staff. Not in London.'

'Well, my dear, we do have a bit more than that, what with rents, the stables, and my brother's interests in the City, but somehow I rather envy your situation. Country life can be deadly boring at times. There is very little that happens here, even when you're the sister of the Earl of Muntglare. There are so few eligible gentlemen in this region.' Eligible gentlemen? Did I care about that shortage? I rather thought that I did not.

Suzanne removed her jacket and hung it on the back of a chair. She was wearing a white, high-necked shirtwaist under it. Quite a practical choice, I thought. My dress buttoned up the back, so I needed the help of a maid to get in or out of it. Suzanne's shirtwaist buttoned in the front. She had it off, and had laid it across the same chair, in no time at all. I couldn't help thinking that she looked rather fetching in her corset and skirt.

'Could you help me with this dress?' I asked, turning my back towards her.

'Of course.' She stepped close and began to undo the buttons. There seemed to be a ridiculous number of them to undo, as there always were, but at last they were all undone and I was able to slip out of the bodice.

Our skirts didn't require any help. Both of us could reach those buttons, and we soon found ourselves standing there in corset, shift, stockings, and boots. Boots and stocking went next, then corsets. Suzanne, ever practical wore a front-lace style she could put on and remove herself. Mine, like my dress, was laced up the back and required assistance. Still, with a little help from Suzanne, it was removed.

I walked over to the door and shut off the gas to the sconces. The low paraffin flames in the bedside lamps cast only a dim glow over the room.

'Time for some rest,' I said, pulling back the counterpane and sheets.

Suzanne climbed into bed with me. We had frequently slept together in school, particularly on cold nights, when the fire in the hearth only just managed to keep the chill at bay. The bed in my room is, naturally, a good bit larger than the narrow cots we'd had at school. Roomy enough for two to sleep there without bumping into each other.

As we settled in, Suzanne rolled over and draped an arm across me. 'Do you remember the things we used to do on those cold nights at school?' she asked, giggling.

'I do, indeed,' I replied.

'I wondered if you did,' she went on. 'This is a big house, and I am sure you have an empty bedroom or two for guests, yet instead you suggest sharing your room and bed with me.'

'I like having company,' I explained. Suzanne's hand was resting on my breast. That brought back pleasant memories of those cold nights at school. Sharing body warmth. Holding each other close, our hands so comforting, bare flesh against bare flesh.

'So do I,' she whispered. 'When it's you.'

She leaned over me, her lips brushing mine, lingering, barely touching. The hand on my breast was gently kneading the sensitive flesh. I could feel my nipple growing harder, pressing against her palm.

I reached up, putting my arms around her, pulling her closer. Her lips pressed tighter against mine, her tongue sliding out, finding my own, the soft yet firm penetration so delightful, as ever it had been. I had one hand on her arse, my fingers working, pulling up the soft fabric of her night dress until they were touching the pale, rounded flesh.

'Do you remember that thing we used to do?' she asked, momentarily breaking off from our frantic kissing and caressing.

'I remember a *lot* of things we used to do," I laughed, my hand still kneading her naked arse.

Suzanne giggled prettily. 'I think we may be over-dressed.'

I nodded agreement. We broke apart for the few moments it required to shed our night dresses, so that we were revealed in our natural glory in the dim glow of the lamps.

Suzanne is such a lovely girl. She stands only two inches over five feet tall, two inches shorter than me, and I would be very much surprised to find she weighs more than eight stone, or even that much. Her breasts are lovely, high and firm, with hard, dark nipples that still show some of the puffiness of youth. As we were ready for bed, her coppery-red hair was loose, falling halfway down her back. In the lamplight, the dense red patch covering her mound was like fire.

With a firm but gentle touch, Suzanne pushed me back on the bed, so that I was lying flat on my back. Carefully, she lifted one leg over me, so that she was straddling me, facing away from me. She leaned down, bringing her lovely quim just above my chin, while I could feel her fingers at work on my own, parting the sensitive lips before she dipped her head and began to lick at the tingling bud within.

I pulled her down closer, began to lick her inviting pink slit. She still tasted quite as good as she had when we were students. I am somewhat fond of the pungent taste of spunk, but, to be honest, I love the taste of an aroused woman's quim even more. To have my tongue buried in a lover's cunt while she is tonguing mine is quite the most wonderful experience I can imagine. One I have mostly neglected since leaving school, as it was obvious I could not bring my lovely Suzanne with me, but had to be satisfied with having her on those rare occasions when she could visit. Too rare, really, for this was the first time we had been intimate together since our graduation.

My body was trembling all over as Suzanne's ever-talented tongue sent erotic sensations shooting through my body like electric sparks. It was all I could do to keep from crying out in ecstasy as I began to climax.

I feel so wicked writing all of this in my journal. I am sure it is fortunate that I use my own private cipher to write, for it would be embarrassing in the extreme should anyone but me ever be able to read this. I try to be completely honest within these pages, something not really expected, or accepted, in a woman.

Thoroughly satisfied, we soon fell asleep in each other's arms, as we had so often done on those cold winter's nights at school. We did not bother to put on our night dresses again, hoping, perhaps, that when we rose for breakfast we could have each other as the first course.

II: Suzanne Willis's Diary

Wednesday, 3rd July — I think I shall have to adopt my darling Anna's habit of writing her diary in a private code. There is so much I want to set down here, yet I know my dear mother sometimes manages to read this, and I would not wish to scandalise her. For now, though, not having the time or patience to devise my own system on the spot, I shall simply switch to writing this in the Pitman short-hand we learned in school. I know my mother cannot read it, though it will not conceal my thoughts from Anna, who is quite as proficient as I, or from any other short-hand reader. I really must work out a less obvious cipher.

I slept very soundly, once we two had satisfied our hungers. It was well past dawn when we arose. Anna rang for O'Leary — her Christian name, Anna tells me, is Maureen, a lovely Irish lass from Balbriggan — and, as she had promised, she had ironed my wrinkled dresses. Having a proper lady's maid was a great help for Anna, whose clothing is both luxurious and awkward to manage without aid. I am not so reliant on servants for these things, so I was quite able to dress myself. One must simply avoid anything that fastens in the back.

Last night brought back many pleasant memories of school. I fear I was never a particularly good student, and, for the most part, never cared for school. But sharing a room with Anna was quite another thing. If I loathed my lessons, I adored my roommate.

I still quite vividly recall the first time we slept together. It was a bitter cold December night, just a week after my eighteenth birthday, and even with extra coal on the fire our room was still quite chilly. My darling Anna — she had forbidden me to address her as "Lady Anna" when we were alone, arguing that formality had no place between best friends — suggested that I join her on her cot, where we could share our bodily warmth.

'It will help keep us warm,' she told me.

I was chilled, so I readily agreed to the experiment. I climbed into her narrow bed and snuggled up to her.

'It might be better,' she suggested, 'if we remove our night dresses. Bare skin certainly transfers more heat than thick wool.'

She was correct. We removed our night dresses, spreading them atop the blankets, where they might provide a bit of additional cover. I was warmer almost at once, with our naked bodies pressed against each other under the covers.

What followed was astonishing. Somehow, we began kissing. I think darling Anna said something about never having kissed a boy, and wondering what it felt like. I lacked that experience as well, but was certainly willing to experiment with her. It was too cold in our room to get truly creative, but we spent a long time teaching each other how to kiss, letting the sensations take over. Our hands explored each other's bodies, and I absolutely thrilled when my darling's fingers began to explore my nether regions.

Over the rest of that final year, we were constantly experimenting, finding new ways to bring each other to a shattering climax. We knew we were wicked to be doing these things, of course, but we didn't care. What society doesn't know, society cannot condemn. The first time Anna began to tongue my pretty pink quim I knew that this was something I wanted to happen as often as possible.

So it was a special delight last night—or, perhaps, I should say this morning—to find us once again naked in the same bed. Being a warm night, we could push the sheets and blankets down to the foot of the big bed, so that we might gaze lovingly upon each other's nude forms in the soft, dim lamplight. Anna is such an exquisite beauty, with her slender frame and large, beautiful breasts, and her long, silky blond hair falling down her back, or spread behind her on the pillow.

One who knew her only casually might think her a bit aloof, with the haughtiness that comes of being the daughter of a peer. I know her much more intimately, and what she reveals when we are alone is nothing at all like the façade she presents to strangers. With me, she is warm and loving. She is my dearest friend, and a wonderful lover.

Later— There was a most curious incident in the stables to-day. I was walking with Anna in the early afternoon, and our route brought us to the stables. It might have been a lovely day for a ride, had we been appropriately dressed.

We entered the stables to examine the horses, as we certainly intended to ride at some time during my visit. We were attracted by a rhythmic grunting and pounding sound from the box at the far end, so, being curious, we walked over there to see what it was.

It proved to be one of the grooms, who had a kitchen maid bent over a bale of fodder, with her skirts up on her back. He was vigorously plunging his impressive member in and out of her quim, and she was just as energetically pushing back against him.

The box was closed, and we were looking in through a wide space between two boards in the door. We could see them, as they coupled inside, but they could not see us. It allowed us to watch, fascinated. As I said, the groom was quite handsomely endowed, and his big organ glistened in the light of a box window from the maid's sweet juices.

The maid was moaning loudly now, her breath catching, becoming ragged, and I knew just from the sound that she was in the midst of a lovely climax. Unable to resist, I found myself hiking up my skirts and slipping a finger into my own succulent cunt.

Beside me, Anna was doing the same. It would have been a fascinating scene to an outsider, two young women outside a box stall, peering through a crack in the door, each with a hand holding her privates, rubbing them, seeking relief from the sexual tension generated by watching the two servants who were fucking inside the box.

I put my left arm around Anna's slender waist, pulling her closer to me. She put her right arm around me in response. Allowing her skirts to drop back down for a moment, she placed her free hand on top of mine as I diddled myself. I carefully removed my hand, allowing her to take over, and freeing that hand to lift up her skirts and insert a finger into her moist, fragrant centre.

We had to leave ourselves unsatisfied, for just about then the groom groaned loudly and thrust hard into the maid's cunt. From the way his body was jerking, I could tell that he was climaxing. I knew it would be a matter of only a few seconds, certainly no longer than a minute, before he had hoisted up his trousers and emerged from the stall. We beat a hasty retreat from the stable and resumed our walk.

Looking back when we were two or three hundred yards from the stable, we saw the maid hurry out and rush back to the house. We did not see the groom emerge, and I presumed that was because he was already in his workplace.

We continued to the Old House, unused since the New Lodge was built. It was a big, rather eerie-looking place, built in the half-timbered style popular during the Tudor period.

'Most of the façade was built during the reign of Richard III, and the oldest part was erected in the eleventh century,' Anna informed me. 'There is absolutely nothing modern about the place. When we still lived here, when I was still a small child, it was hot in the summer and cold and draughty if the winter. If you wanted to bathe, you used an iron tub in the kitchen. Chamber pots took care of other needs. I do not miss it.'

I thought of the luxurious bathrooms in the New Lodge. Her opinion was understandable.

Still, we ventured inside. Most of the furnishings had been moved to the New Lodge, but a few rooms retained their fixtures. The library walls were still lined with shelves, now empty, the books transported to new shelves in the new house. Cushions remained on the window seat, however, presumably because they would not have fit had they been moved. We sat down upon them and looked out through the thick, diamond-paned leaded windows, across a vast expanse of green lawn, and into the dense woodland beyond.

Who could say what the occupants had once seen through those windows? Had Yorkist and Lancastrian armies once marched past? Or paused to camp for the night, or to fight some minor skirmish as Henry Tudor sought to wrest control of England from the cruel usurper, Richard, before their final encounter at Bosworth Field?

Now there were only sheep, and a few small, brown cows grazing on the lawn, their munching keeping the grass trimmed.

'I fear we were interrupted before time,' Anna commented, taking my hands in hers. She lifted my right hand to her nose and sniffed at my fingers with a pleased look. She sucked my middle finger into her mouth, sighing contentedly, no doubt tasting herself, for only a few minutes before that finger had been probing deeply in her pretty cunt.

'We were, indeed,' I agreed, leaning forward and kissing her sweet lips. She held me tightly, and we exchanged feverish kisses, sitting there on the window seat, with the warm sun shining upon us through the thick glass.

Both of us were reaching down with one hand, pulling up each other's skirts and petticoats, ever so eager to continue where we had left off in the stable. Anna's sweet cunt was still moist and slick with the dewy nectar of her passion. My fingers slipped easily inside her, probing deeply, even as the heel of my hand pressed and caressed that lovely pink nub wherein lies the centre of a woman's pleasure.

We were, of course, quite aware that what we were doing was 'wrong,' but neither of us cared now any more than we had cared back at school. To hell with propriety was my thought, and I am sure Anna would agree with that proposition. A woman must, naturally, seek a husband, and endure congress with a man, if she wishes to fulfil her natural function as a mother, but the love and passion enjoyed by two women transcends the brief, brutal couplings which seem to be all that men are capable of.

No man can provide intimate service for more than a few minutes, whilst two women are able to enjoy each other, body and soul, for hours upon end, until every nerve, every fibre of their being, has been stimulated and satisfied to the very peak of erotic ecstasy.

I was feeling an incredible upwelling of love and eroticism at just that moment, with Anna's lips pressed sensuously against mine, and her fingers working deep within me. My body was trembling. It was difficult to breath, one prolonged spasm of erotic pleasure following rapidly upon the tail of another.

We confined our play to kissing and touching, for it seemed impractical to fully disrobe in the old house, but that hardly mattered. I cannot recall how many times my body convulsed to a powerful climax, nor how often my darling Anna joined me in that ultimate expression of sensuality. I know only that, by the time we ceased, both of us could hardly rise to our feet, for we were both physically spent to the degree that we could hardly walk, and mentally exhausted, as if extreme pleasure had temporarily dulled all of our senses.

The rest of the day was something of an anti-climax. We walked back to the New Lodge hand in hand. We joined Edwin—I suppose I really should call him Lord Muntglare, but he has always been Edwin to me—for supper. We read in the library for a few hours after supper, fortified by a glass of two of brandy. All quite routine.

Now O'Leary has been in and helped Anna undress. She even insisted upon helping me, though I always make it a practice to dress in a manner than doesn't require any such help. Now she has gone, and Anna has locked the bedroom door and is sitting naked, looking ravishing, on the edge of the bed, looking at me and smiling enticingly.

I think I've written enough for this day.

III: Lord Muntglare's Journal

Thursday, 4th July— Anna's school friend is a welcome addition to the household. I shall enjoy having her here for the next few weeks. She seems a delightful young woman, full of vigour and good cheer. She is also quite lovely. I must admit a weakness for red hair, and hers is that alluring shade of coppery red which, combined with her milky complexion and wonderful figure, must make her the amorous target of every man she encounters. My sister is a beauty, but Suzanne is stunning.

I spoke to my sister shortly after Suzanne arrived and enquired if the two of them might consent to my taking a few photographs of them. Anna has modelled for me on many occasions, and is familiar with my skills, which, I like to believe, are of quite a high level. It would not do to exhibit my photographs, of course, yet I think they are the equal of any produced by photographic artists of the plebeian sort.

Anna spoke with Suzanne and gained her assent. We were to take the first photographs to-day, in the studio our father had attached to the building when he erected the New Lodge. It is a lovely space, quite large, high up in the house with a huge window set into the north-facing gable that provides a perfect, even light. Father intended it as an artist's studio, for he was a marvellous painter. Anna still sometimes uses it for its original purpose. She is by no means a painter of Father's calibre, but she is certainly capable of some lovely water-colours. Father, truth be told, could certainly have made a very comfortable living as a portraitist, had there been any need for him to do so.

I have a number of fine cameras, but the two I planned to use to-day are a Lancaster & Son Instantograph view camera, using eight by ten-inch dry plates, and a Kodak stereoscopic camera. My equipment is quite up to date, especially when I compare it to that I first learnt to use only a few years ago. Today, one may purchase dry plates on a celluloid base already prepared, and so sensitive that a mechanical shutter mechanism is required to capture an image. The days of wet plates and seconds-long exposures are over, and the photographer is far better for it.

Anna and Suzanne appeared at breakfast in loose fitting dresses, with their hair merely pinned up, but not fully dressed. I had proposed taking a series of informal portraits and stereographic views, wherein the pair would be portrayed as simple country maidens.

After breakfast, we adjourned to the studio. The sky was bright, but slightly overcast, and the diffused north light shining through the great windows was perfect for my purpose.

At first, I had each of them, in turn, sit upon a tall stool, turned to the side, but with their heads turned towards the camera, and took several exposures of their beautiful faces. They had let their hair down now. I found myself wishing I could take colour photographs, for Suzanne's coppery hair was especially beautiful in the north light. It made me wish that I had taken the trouble to learn the art of hand-colouring photographs.

When this was accomplished, I withdrew to my dark-room for a few minutes. I removed the plates from the holders and transferred them to my light-safe. I then loaded the holder with new plates, closed the dark slides, and returned to the studio ready to take more exposures.

Anna was helping Suzanne out of her dress. My dear sister was already nude. I sometimes fear there is a bit of the exhibitionist in her nature. Suzanne seemed only slightly more modest, smiling prettily at me as her dress slid down her body and pooled about her feet. I had asked them to forgo under-garments, which have an unfortunate way of leaving unsightly marks upon the nude body that can take hours to fade completely.

With both young women nude, I began to pose them on a *papier mâché* landscape I had built in my studio. They would appear to be lounging upon a rocky hillside, though, in fact, they were comfortably posed in a dry, congenial studio. I have taken many photographs of my beautiful sister posed upon these pseudo boulders. Some, where she is clothed, I have enlarged and placed about the house. Those where she is nude, of course, are kept secure from the eyes of strangers, as will be the views I take to-day.

I posed Anna lying back upon a large boulder, one shoulder raised, to allow her to face the camera. Suzanne was seated in front of her, and Anna rested one hand upon her friend's thigh. Suzanne was leaning towards my sister, gazing at her in feigned longing, and her lovely breasts, with their small, dark nipples, were proudly displayed to my indirect gaze as I focused the image on the ground-glass screen. I inserted a film holder, exposed it, turned it over, and took a second exposure.

I moved them a bit. Anna remained essentially as she was, but now I had Suzanne move so that she was leaning over my sister, as if they were about to kiss. I had to move her arm slightly, for it was obscuring the camera's view of her lovely breasts, the nipples now hard and brushing against Anna's.

'If you could kiss,' I said, 'I believe it would make a beautiful photograph. If you don't think it too risqué, that is.'

'Not at all,' Anna declared.

Suzanne smiled and shook her head. 'Just tell us when you are ready,' she said.

I moved the camera, on its heavy wooden tripod, into position, ducked under the black cloth hood, and carefully composed the image and focused the camera. I emerged from under the hood, inserted a loaded film holder, and nodded to Suzanne.

'I am ready,' I said.

She smiled and lowered her head. Their lips touched, gently, sensuously, came together harder as I tripped the shutter. They continued to kiss as I reversed the film holder and took a second shot. I saw my sister's hand move downward, her fingers playing in the nest of fiery red hair that adorned Suzanne's mound. I got back under the hood, recomposed, and grabbed another fresh film holder.

You cannot focus and load a large view camera too quickly. By the time I was ready to snap the shutter again, Suzanne was fondling Anna's blond-framed cunt as well. I was working under a bit of a handicap now, for my own masculine member was responding to the images in front of me, making a conspicuous bulge in my trousers.

I took two more photographs, then put aside the big view camera and picked up the Kodak. I had equipped this with a range-finder that used a split prism to determine distance. This allowed me to set the focus much faster than on a cumbersome ground glass. It also allowed me to hold the camera, rather than having to mount it upon a tripod. The composition was obviously less precise, looking through an eye-hole and a rectangular wire frame and not a ground glass screen that exactly matched the film, but it was accurate enough.

The two women seemed to be improvising. It was as if they had forgotten I was in the studio with them. They were kissing passionately, holding each other close with one arm whilst, with the hand of the other, each rubbed and probed at the others most secret parts.

I snapped all of twenty images with the stereoscopic camera before setting it aside. There were no more unused film holders for either camera, and I could not bear to return to the dark-room whilst these two lovely damsels were so intimately engaged.

Now Suzanne began to stir. She crept downward, her lips trailing across my dear sister's throat, lingering to kiss, and tease, and suck at Anna's hard pink nipples, and trail down across her flat stomach and through the blond thatch of pubic hair. She began to lick at Anna's beautiful cunt, her pink tongue laving the whole length of my sister's nether lips.

I could resist no longer. I found myself unbuttoning my trousers and pulling out my swollen member. Doctor Kellogg and his sort might quietly go to Hades, for all I cared at that moment. I watched the two women, rapt, and began to slowly stroke my rock-hard erection.

Anna looked over at me and smiled, laughing softly. I moved closer, my hand moving smoothly up and down on the turgid shaft.

Anna reached down, pulling Suzanne's face more tightly against her golden-haired cleft. I was standing quite close now, and Suzanne's lovely back and shapely bum provided a sensuous backdrop for my stroking.

I could last only a few minutes. I like to think of myself as stoic, a proper, upright, Victorian gentleman, but my senses had been too much assaulted by the sensuous imagery of these two beauties making love to each other. I barely stifled a groan as my manhood began to jerk involuntarily and I shot a huge load of spunk onto the lovely Suzanne's back, some of the pearly droplets splashing into her blazing hair, like jewels against the coppery background.

I honestly do not think that Suzanne even noticed, so intensely was she ministering to my beautiful sister. As my manhood began to shrink, I walked behind her, to find that Suzanne was frantically fingering herself.

I grabbed every one of the film holders and dashed into the dark-room. Rather than reload the holders, I picked up my travel camera, a folding Kodak, and hurried back into the studio. I managed to snap several pictures of Suzanne's red-bordered treasure, her fingers probing deeply, the sweet juices flowing copiously. Ah, if it were only possible to capture the motion, the ecstatic moans and sighs as she climaxed.

I did snap three photographs of Anna as she writhed in her fulfilment, hoping there was enough light for the high shutter speed, 1/50th of a second, that I employed.

Later— I have developed and fixed all the negatives, and made prints and stereographs from the best of them. It was a most productive day in the studio, I must say. I set up the photographs in the studio, knowing that Anna and Suzanne will certainly wish to view them before I lock them away, out of sight of the hoi polloi. We are a separate breed, we of the ancient peerage, and need not be concerned with the terribly conventional morality of those who surround us.

Yet, at the same time, we must also be conscious of appearances. We dare not allow these little foibles of ours to become common knowledge. The peasantry lack discernment. If the lady of the manor—which, at least until one of us marries, my sister is by default, both of our parents having departed this mortal coil—wishes to allow herself to be photographed *en déshabille,* or in intimate congress with a female companion, what does it matter to the local yeomanry? They would only disapprove, in their narrow-minded way. What we do must stay private.

Anna and Suzanne have now viewed today's work and most heartily approve. I have therefore locked the photographs away, save for those selected by Suzanne to carry home. I will make reduced-size prints of those. Except for the portraits, those poses she selected are not those where either woman might easily be identified.

As for me, it is now well past my normal bed-time, so I must conclude writing here.

IV: Albert Morgan's Journal

Friday, 5th July — It is nearly midnight, and as I make it a fixed duty to write in this journal every day, without fail, I must set this down before I retire for the night. This day was little different from any other until it was very nearly time to close the office and return home. At ten minutes before five o'clock, a messenger entered the office with a telegram, addressed to 'Principal Agent, Morgan & Sons, Estate Agents.'

Upon my assurance that I was, indeed, the senior Mr. Morgan, the messenger handed me the telegram. I read through it quickly, in case there was need of a reply, then sent the boy on his way, with tuppence for his trouble.

The telegram itself was short and to the point:

WILL ARRIVE YOUR OFFICE 9 PM. APOLOGISE FOR INCONVENIENCE. INTER-
ESTED IN PURCHASING WINSTEAD. RAVENSBROOK.

It was a bit cryptic, in that I had no idea who this Ravensbrook might be. I hardly cared. The Winstead estate had been a problem ever since the owners placed it on my list. It was an ancient place, looking rather like it belonged in a Poe or Collins tale. While not actually a castle, for it was built in 1656, during Cromwell's so-called Protectorate, it was designed to resemble an old Norman fortified manor house. It was the sort of place you expected to be under siege, and as no effort had ever been exerted to modern-ise the old house, I was finding it very difficult to sell.

The owners live in London, and their only concern is that I get no less that £15,000 for the property. A great deal of money, obviously, even when one considers that the old house sits on twenty-seven acres of parkland and forest, and I am sure is why I have thus far had no luck in selling the place. Were it left to me, I should have set the price at somewhere around £8,000.

The mysterious Mr. Ravensbrook arrived precisely on time. He was a tall man, I should say about thirty-years-old, with dark hair and cold, grey eyes. He had the look of one who rarely ventured out into the sunlight.

He was dressed conservatively, in a brown tweed suit and black bowler hat, and carried a quite distinctive ebony walking stick, with a gold top in the shape of an eagle's head.

'Mr. Ravensbrook?' I enquired.

'*Lord* Ravensbrook, actually,' he said, smiling and extending his hand.

I shook his hand, then led him into my private office. I had the Winstead file on my desk.

'You are interested in purchasing the Winstead estate, I believe?' I said.

'Exactly.'

'I trust you realise that the owners are very firm, and will entertain no offer of less than £15,000.'

'And would, no doubt, be even more pleased were the offer larger,' Ravensbrook commented. 'Well, it won't be. But £15,000 is quite acceptable, presuming the estate passes my inspection.'

'And when would you like to examine the property, your lordship?'

'To-night, if that's not too inconvenient. Of an evening, in any case. I am rather a nocturnal person, you see.

I have extremely sensitive skin, and burn from even the slightest exposure to the sun.'

'That must be terribly inconvenient,' I offered.

Ravensbrook nodded gravely. 'Oh, very. It means I must conduct my business at night, or go about so heavily swathed and shrouded that people find my appearance quite disturbing. No, it is better to simply live by night.'

I was forced to agree. It would obviously be difficult for a man with such a malady to get about during the day. Nor did I have any objection to showing him the property, even so late in the evening.

'My only question, my lord, is whether you will be able to fully appreciate the house and grounds without the sun to illuminate it? Surely that must pose a problem?'

'No, good sir,' the peer replied. 'The moon is nearly full, and the night is clear. And I find that I can see almost as well in bright moonlight as others see in full daylight. Perhaps a sort of strange compensation for my skin condition? I see better in a dim light than a bright one. And, of course, when I look at a house, I find I am less concerned with its exterior aspect than with the interior. One doesn't really live in the garden, does one?'

'No,' I said, 'I suppose not. In any event, I am at your disposal, if you would care to look at the property to-night.'

'Excellent. My coach is waiting at the kerb.'

Oh, I travelled in style on that visit. The coach was a neat, four-horse black Berlin, with the Ravensbrook coat of arms painted on the doors. The lord took the forward-facing seat, whilst I elected to sit opposite him. The elderly coachman, it appeared, was familiar with the property and knew how to get there.

It took some time to drive out to the Winstead estate, which was situated well out in the country. The nearest neighbour is Lord Muntglare's estate. The two properties adjoin, separated by a high stone wall and dense woods, which preserve the privacy of both.

'This is excellent,' Lord Ravensbrook declared, as we alighted from the coach. 'One can almost imagine battles raging about the walls, with staunch Royalists within and a pack of Roundheads without.'

'Unfortunately for that romantic image, your lordship, the house wasn't built until 1656. If there were any battles in the Civil War fought here, they would have been fought in an open field.'

The moon was quite bright. It would be full on the morrow. There was no problem at all finding our way about the grounds, which we explored for a few minutes before entering the house. This was where I expected problems to arise.

As I noted, no effort was ever made to modernise the place. That meant, among other inconveniences, that there was no gas lighting. We had to find our way around the empty rooms by the light of a pair of bull's-eye lanterns I had brought along.

'You will have to use paraffin lamps, I'm afraid,' I said. 'There is no gas installed.'

'I expected as much. Surely the gas lines have not been extended this far out into the country?'

I had to tell him they had not been. 'Lord Muntglare, whose estate adjoins this,' I offered, 'has his own gas works, however, so if you'd care to install gas lighting, perhaps you could prevail upon him to become your supplier.'

'More likely, I will simply use lamps and candles. I find dim lighting works best in old houses. The faults are less obvious. In any event, I believe this house will suit my needs most admirably.'

'Will you make an offer, then, my lord?'

'They may have their £15,000,' he answered. 'Provided the title can be transferred no later than a week from the coming Monday.'

'I am sure that can be managed.'

'Excellent. Shall we return to your office and draw up the necessary documents?'

I see by my watch that it is nearly midnight, so I will draw today's journal to a close. The papers have been drawn up and the purchase contract signed. I will take the morning train to London to finalise the sale.

V: Suzanne Willis's Diary

Thursday, 11th July — Much excitement today. All day long, carters were hauling great waggon loads of furniture, draperies, and other necessary things to the ancient, empty house on the adjoining estate. The story in the village is that the estate has been sold to a marquess, and is being told with some amusement, for, if true, this would mean that Edwin, an earl, is no longer the highest-ranking peer in the county.

Young O'Leary, who seems to be well connected to the local rumour mongers, has related the oddest tale of this new owner. He is said to be in some way quite allergic to sunlight, so that he lives a strange, nocturnal existence. O'Leary informed us that she had the news from a friend, coming from the same village in Ireland, who is in service to the elder Mr. Morgan, the estate agent, who arranged the sale of the estate.

'He is said to be quite handsome,' O'Leary informed us, 'but very pale.'

'You really mustn't gossip, O'Leary,' Anna admonished, after a moment adding, 'Unless it's to us, naturally.'

'Of course, my lady.'

'But do tell us more,' I encouraged. Anna nodded vigorously in agreement.

'There's not much more to tell, I'm afraid, mum. That was all Kathleen could learn from her employer. Mr. Morgan is not the most talkative of men, to hear her tell the tale.'

Pity, I thought. This new neighbour sounded an interesting sort.

'What do you hear about his household?' Anna asked. 'Surely there will be positions for some of the village people?'

'I've heard nothing so far,' O'Leary replied. 'Perhaps he's bringing staff with him. No one seems to know if he's moving his entire household into Winstead, or if it will simply be a country retreat and he will spend the bulk of his time elsewhere.'

'We shall have to learn more,' I suggested to Anna.

'We shall, indeed.'

Later— I have now met Lord Ravensbrook, and I am very much impressed. He despatched an elderly servant after Tea, to enquire if his master might call upon us this evening after the sun had set. The servant was properly reticent, but did confirm that his master was terribly allergic to the sun, and so generally preferred to socialise only after sunset. Edwin naturally offered his hospitality, and it was arranged that Lord Ravensbrook should come at nine o'clock.

I was quite impressed by him. He arrived, in a magnificent black Berlin, promptly upon the hour. He was quite tall, at least two inches above six feet, his height even more impressive as he walked from his coach with his tall silk hat still on his head. He doffed this as he approached, seeing Anna and I standing there with Edwin to greet him.

He was dressed, as was Edwin, in a proper tailcoat, waistcoat, starched shirtfront, and white bow tie. It being well after dark, he wore a black opera cape over his dress suit, and his hands were covered by white kid gloves. He also carried a stick, a magnificent ebony stick, topped with a gold eagle's head, and with a gold ferrule protecting the tip.

'Anthony,' he said, by way of introduction, 'Marquess Ravensbrook.'

'And I am Edwin Corwin,' Edwin replied, 'Earl of Muntglare. Very pleased to make your acquaintance, your lordship.' He turned to us. 'And, may I present my sister, Lady Anna, and her good friend, Miss Suzanne Willis?'

Ravensbrook smiled at this, bowing slightly. 'Lady Anna,' he said. 'Miss Willis. It is always a pleasure to meet two such beautiful young women. I hope we shall have the opportunity to meet often, now that we are to be neighbours.'

'*We* shall be neighbours, your lordship,' Anna replied. 'Suzanne, sadly, will be here only a few more days. She resides in London.'

'Ah. Then I hope she will permit me to call upon her when I am in the city. I intend to live at Winstead, to be sure, but no doubt I will have to visit my London residence to attend to business from time to time.'

'It would be a pleasure, your lordship,' I assured him. 'I will look forward to it.'

Edwin led us inside. A footman took Lord Ravensbrook's hat, stick, and cape, and Edwin led us all into the front parlour, a comfortable little room furnished for receiving company. Anna and I took seats on the little settee, whilst the two men each took one of the comfortable, overstuffed leather armchairs that faced it. Anna and I would remain for a few minutes, after which we would naturally withdraw and leave the men to talk of sport, or shooting, or whatever it is that men talk of once the ladies have withdrawn.

Now that we were indoors, in a better light, I took the opportunity to get a better look at our guest. Lord Ravensbrook was quite handsome, though rather pale from his nocturnal existence. His eyes were pale grey, whilst his longish hair, which he wore combed straight back from his high forehead, was a very dark brown, looking almost black from the oil he used to dress it.

O'Leary had already informed us, based upon the local gossip, though evidently obtained from someone who had been inside his new home and learnt it from the butler, that he was 27-years-old and, interestingly, unmarried.

That would no doubt be of more interest to Anna than to me, even if he *had* indicated he would like to call upon me in London. She is, after all, Lady Anna Corwin, daughter of the 17th Earl of Muntglare and sister of the 18th Earl. I really had no idea of how far back Lord Ravensbrook's title descended, but the daughter of an earl was certainly a better match for a marquess than the daughter of a deceased barrister, even of a barrister who was made Queen's Counsel four years before his passing.

I never felt common around Anna, and her brother always treated me with the utmost respect, but they were of the peerage and I was not. She would certainly have first choice of this handsome young nobleman, should she so wish.

We withdrew after half an hour of small talk and retired to our room.

'He is very handsome,' I commented.

'Fine for you, dear,' Anna said. 'There's something about him that disturbs me.' She shook her head prettily. 'I really don't know what it might be, but there is something.'

'I find him fascinating. He certainly seems well-travelled, particularly for not yet having attained his thirtieth year.'

'Yes, he does seem to be that.' Anna shook her head again, looking across the room at me from her perch on the window-seat. The moon, still about three-quarters full, shone through the open window, casting a pale, blue light across the garden below. 'Oh, Suzanne, I really don't know what it is about him I mistrust. Perhaps it is simply his manner. Doesn't he seem, well, older than his years? I know he is but twenty-seven, yet he seems so settled, so serene, as if he were grown weary of life, though it has hardly begun. He is older than us, but not that much.'

I thought about what she said. Lord Ravensbrook did, indeed, seem somehow older, wiser, than most men of his years.

'I have a friend,' I suggested, 'Camille, whose brother is a pursuivant at the College of Arms. I could write to her and we should be able to learn all there is to know about Lord Ravensbrook.'

'I have a better idea,' Anna said. 'Or, at least, a more expedient one. Wait here, I shan't be a moment.'

She left the room and was gone for several minutes, returning with a book. 'This is only the 1892 edition, I fear,' she said, handing me the book, 'but it should still serve.'

It was a copy of Burke's *Peerage*. The Marquess Ravensbrook would certainly be listed.

We found the entry quickly enough. It was an old title, originally bestowed upon one Anthony Ravensbrook, at that time Baron Pumberly and Viscount Llandoludd, in 1486 by King Henry VII. Curiously, the eldest son in each generation was always named Anthony, so it seemed that there had never been a Marquess Ravensbrook who bore a different name from his predecessor. Burke listed the incumbent as Anthony Ravensbrook, aged 89 in 1892, and having one son, at that time using the courtesy title Viscount Llandoludd—which, Anna informs me, is pronounced 'Yan-duh-liff,' curse the Welsh and their ridiculous language—and who was now, presumably, the Lord Ravensbrook who sat chatting with Edwin in the front parlour.

Since his father was still alive when this edition of Burke's was published, there was no way of knowing just when, over the past three years, our new friend had inherited the title.

'This doesn't tell us very much,' I said, 'except that he is the 15th Marquess Ravensbrook, and that he seems to come from a remarkably long-lived family. I believe I shall still write to Camille. She may be able to throw some additional light onto the subject.'

'Long-lived is certainly true, for his title dates to 1486, more than a hundred years before the Muntglare title, yet my brother is the 18th earl, whilst he is only the 15th marquess. In addition to every Marquess Ravensbrook having the same Christian name, they all seem to live well past eighty.'

There was a gentle tapping at the bedchamber door about this time. Anna rose to answer it. She found O'Leary standing in the corridor.

'Lord Ravensbrook is about to depart, Lady Anna,' she reported. 'Your brother has asked that you and Miss Willis join him to say "farewell."'

We followed O'Leary downstairs, finding the two men in the entry hall.

We made our good-byes, and Lord Ravensbrook was off in his lovely coach.

Anna and I returned to our room a few minutes later. I shall have to leave off writing now. She has a most enticing look in her eyes, and has again asked me to help her undress. I can only hope this night is as delightful as the others have been thus far during this visit.

VI: Lady Anna Corwin's Journal

Friday, 12th July— A very strange night. Suzanne and I retired to bed shortly after midnight. She was my same wonderful Suzanne, lavishing my quim with her full attention. How lovely her tongue feels as it probes my tender, quivering flesh. And how delicious she is, when I reciprocate. I could lick her beautiful, pink cunt forever and never tire of the taste, or of the little noises she makes as she allows her wonderful body to throw off the restraints of propriety and give in to the sheer delight of love-making.

As always since Suzanne has been here, we fell asleep in each other's arms, the bedside lamps burning low, putting out just enough light for me to appreciate the beauty of my sweet lover's form, and thrill to the way the dim light shines through her coppery hair.

It was well after midnight when I awakened. This struck me as rather odd, for I have been the soundest of sleepers since childhood. Nothing ever wakes me.

Yet there I was, lying in bed, my lover's arm draped across me, suddenly quite awake, yet unable to move.

I am not sure just why, but I felt that we were not alone in the room. That idea at once seemed quite silly. The door was locked. No one could get in that way. The house was less than twenty-years-old, so there was no question of secret passages within the wall that would allow someone to slip in and out unnoticed. If there were, I'd have seen them being constructed and would know all about them.

I hesitate to write what follows. It seems too fantastical, too *outré*, too strange, to have really happened, though I have the evidence before me in the glass as I write.

The room was still dimly lit by the bedside lamps. It seemed hazy, as if a dank fog had somehow penetrated into the room. Or perhaps smoky, though there was no smell of smoke.

Then, very slowly, I noticed the haze taking form. Indistinct at first, it slowly formed into a face, hovering over the bed, looking down on me. I should have felt very conscious of my nudity, yet somehow it didn't seem to matter. Rather than try to cover myself, an act almost instinctual in any well brought up young woman, I rolled onto my back, my arms flung wide, my legs well apart, as if I were showing off the most intimate parts of me to the hovering face.

I am dreaming, I thought. My intimacy with Suzanne has conceived a somnolent fantasy, in which our new neighbour seems to have been included. For it was Lord Ravensbrook's face which was floating above me, smiling benignly, making me ache with carnal desire.

The mist seemed to coalesce at the foot of the bed. In my dream, it seemed as if the marquess himself was standing there, quite naked, his rampant manhood thrust out before him.

He climbed upon the bed. I drew up my legs, spread my knees well apart, as he lowered himself above me. His massive member pressed at the portal of my quim, insisting it be allowed to enter. I knew this was wrong, but it was a dream, and dreams are to be enjoyed in the moment, and agonised over only in the light of day. The dreaming 'me' simply pulled her legs up higher and wrapped them around his back, pulling that magnificent organ deep into her cunt.

As he began to thrust, I could feel the pleasure radiating up from within. My body craved the attention. His member was so big that it was almost painful as he rogered me, yet I cared not at all. In my dream, pain was not something to be dreaded, but to be embraced.

His lips pressed against mine. We exchanged deep, passionate kisses. Dreamily, I was aware of my loving Suzanne lying on her side, facing me, her head propped up on her hand, watching me with a strange, interested expression.

So, she was in my dream as well, I thought. Even more lovely. Perhaps she would join in the fun?

Lord Ravensbrook's kisses covered my face. His lips brushed the sensitive skin of my throat. I felt a slight twinge where his mouth covered my neck, but any such sensation was overwhelmed as his giant member began to pulse, spewing what seemed like gallons of spunk into my fertile womb.

And then he was gone. One moment he was there, seemingly corporeal, and the next that strange mist again filled the room, only to somehow be sucked out the open window and vanish.

When I awakened in the morning, I found Suzanne studying me curiously. 'You must have some very strange, very wonderful dreams,' she said.

I thought about the night just ended. That dream was still vivid, as real as if it had actually happened. 'Sometimes,' I replied.

'I watched you last night. Your legs were drawn up, and your body was reacting as if you were in the midst of a lovely fuck. Your body was rocking, clearly climaxing, and you were kissing someone ever so passionately. Yet, there was no one there. It was as if you were being rogered by a ghost.'

'I remember that,' I admitted. 'That is, I remember you watching me in my dream, but in my dream, I was not alone. I was making love with our new neighbour, Lord Ravensbrook. He seemed quite real, yet you say I was alone?'

'Quite alone.'

'Imagination,' I said, 'is a strange and wonderful thing. It all felt very real.'

Suzanne smiled, looking at me curiously. 'What did you do to your neck?' she asked.

'What do you mean?' I inquired.

'Look in the glass.'

I went to my dressing table and sat down in front of the mirror. I thought I looked quite fetching, though somehow a touch paler than usual. But Suzanne was correct, there was something on my throat. Two tiny red marks, about an inch apart, like pin-pricks. What should I make of that, I wondered.

VII: Letter, Camille Underwood to Suzanne Willis

15th July, Corcoran House

My Dearest Friend,

I received your letter in the morning post Saturday last, and at once contacted my brother. He informs me that the Marquess Ravensbrook, who had previously been known by his father's cadet title, Viscount Llandoludd, was confirmed in his present station upon the death of his father on 17th April 1894. He has, I am told, no known heirs, so the title will become extinct upon his passing, presuming he does not, in the interim, marry and produce a male heir. This is one of those ancient titles, dating from 1486, with a Salic entail than can only be inherited by a man, never by a woman, and no male cousins or other relations are known to exist.

He derives income from the lands associated with the Pumberly and Llandoludd titles, as well as from a large estate gifted to his ancestor upon being raised to marquess, then a country holding, but now incorporated within greater London. As those lands are entailed, he is thus made landlord over some eight square miles which have experienced a great deal of commercial development in the last few decades. I should estimate, from what my brother has told me, that he must have an income of well over £12,000 per annum. If he has taken an interest in you, perhaps you should reciprocate. You could certainly do worse.

I remain, as ever
Your loving friend,
CAMILLE UNDERWOOD

VIII: Maureen O'Leary's Diary

Wednesday, 16th July— Oh, Diary, I have been more than a wee bit lonely of late. Lady Anna is quite taken up with entertaining her school friend, so it seems about all I see of her is when I help her dress and undress, and perhaps a time or two during the day, when she needs something ironed, or has some problem of the sort that sensible people deal with easily, but the nobility are helpless in the face of.

Our new neighbour, Lord Ravensbrook, has called several times since he moved in. He seems to fancy Miss Suzanne. Still, more than once, I have seen him exchange a knowing glance with Lady Anna, as if they were privy to some great secret. I cannot but wonder what it might be.

I had a letter from my mother today, written in her usual unskilled hand. She's a lovely, loving woman, but grew up having no advantages. She is barely literate. At times, she complains that I write too well, yet, if she wished me to remain an unlettered peasant all my life, why did she work so hard to ensure that I would have the best education possible? Oh, I know, she is disappointed that I chose to work as a lady's maid for a noble family, but what was her suggested alternative? That I should enter a convent and become a nun? No, that held no appeal. Days spent in prayer and drudgery? I can have the drudgery without the need of stopping to pray at intervals.

Besides, my friend Bridget went into a convent, and she's told me what it's *really* like, with the bloody priest assigned as her confessor giving a penance of six *ave Marias*, ten *pater nosters*, and one *suge meum penem*. She told me she never minded the rosary, but felt the priest has a most inadequate *penem*, really not at all worth sucking, even if it were a *legitimate* penance and not merely some perversion favoured by her confessor.

I also had a letter from my publisher in London. He tells me that my newest book is selling quite well, despite the market being somewhat limited and clandestine. *The Erotic Adventures of a Lady's Maid* is evidently quite popular with a certain crowd. Popular enough for me to receive a lovely cheque in the amount of £250, which I shall deposit in Crowninshield's Bank on the morrow.

There is a great temptation in having so much money. I could easily leave my position, rent a neat little cottage in the village, and live quite comfortably for several years. Perhaps longer, for my publisher assures me there will be more cheques to follow. He is also asking for a new book, and the quicker done, the sooner he can present it to his perverted readership. Oh, Lord Jesus, but I do love those randy old buggers who may yet make a wealthy woman of me, and, to be sure, of Mary Margaret O'Hara, wanton young authoress, and Cecily Freelove, naughty, silly young thing that she is, with her randy employer and friends constantly pressing their suits, and their rampant manhoods, upon her. My life should only be half as interesting as hers.

No, dear diary, I shall simply deposit the money, and none here shall know of it. I am quite satisfied with my life in this household. Wealth is temporary. If my publisher sells many more books, and I write two or three more that sell just as well, then, perhaps, I shall consider putting in my notice and retiring from service to spend my days at a desk, creating more erotic worlds full of over-sexed people. Or even, perhaps, I might forsake the erotic world and write some important novel, upon which I might, with perfect contentment, place my *real* name. For now, though, I shall stay where I am and just bask in the knowledge that, should I ever wish to leave, I can easily afford to do so.

The bell is ringing, and I see by the clock on my wall that it is half ten of the evening. Lady Anna will be preparing for bed, and I must tend to her needs.

Later—

> 'And on that cheek, and o'er that brow,
> So soft, so calm, yet eloquent,
> The smiles that win, the tints that glow,
> But tell of days in goodness spent,
> A mind at peace with all below,
> A heart whose love is innocent!'

Ah, but Byron had a way with him, though all say he was a dangerous man to know too intimately.

I have done my evening duty to Lady Anna, and a bit more besides, and am most pleasantly satisfied to have been of service. Aye, and to *be* serviced, for tonight was more like it so often was in the days before Miss Suzanne came to visit.

Lady Anna was partially disrobed when I entered her room. I helped her remove her skirt and petticoats, and then set about unlacing her corset. Miss Suzanne, who was already in her night dress, watched from the bed.

The lacing loosened, I stood in front of Lady Anna and began to unhook her stays. She was looking at me curiously.

'I have been neglecting you of late, have I not, dear Maureen?' she said. I smiled inwardly at this, for when she addresses me by my Christian name, it is usually the prelude to imparting some particularly juicy bit of gossip, or to a more intimate encounter. I do love my mistress, particularly when she takes it into her pretty head to be naughty.

I undid the last hook, pulled off her stays, and carried them to the little table where they were placed next to two other sets. 'You've been busy with your friend, mum,' I replied. 'I've not noticed.'

'Still, it was unkind of me. You are not just a servant, you must know. I think of you as a friend, I honestly do.'

'I'm hardly of the proper social standing to be your friend, mum, no offence. I'm just an ordinary lady's maid.' A wealthy lady's maid, I thought, but that didn't change my status.

'Nevertheless, I should like to give you a special reward this night. So would Suzanne. Do you think we might do that? I feel so sure you would find it quite a pleasant experience.'

I nodded acquiescence. Miss Suzanne got up from where she was seated on the edge of the bed, and together the two gentlewomen removed my clothing. Soon I stood there between them, naked as the day I was born.

They quickly slipped out of the last bits of their own clothing and led me to the bed, bidding my lie on my back in the middle of it. I did as they bid, and one climbed into the bed on either side of me, Miss Suzanne to my left, Lady Anna to my right. They bent over me together, each of them swirling her tongue around a nipple, sucking it between their soft lips. Lady Anna, who knew me *very* well, nipped lightly with her teeth.

I could feel two hands parting my legs, gentle fingers spreading my nether lips, caressing my secret places, causing me to gasp in surprise at the delightful sensations.

Miss Suzanne trailed kisses down my body and began to tongue my delighted quim. Lady Anna began to kiss me on the mouth. Our mouths opened, and our tongues played their sensual game, just as they used to do.

'Let me taste you,' I whispered. 'Let me lick the sweet nectar from your lovely cunt.'

She sat up, pulled herself up, and straddled my face, lowering her quim to my mouth. I set about tonguing her eagerly. It had been too long.

Tonguing my mistress's beautiful cunt felt wonderful, as did the sensations radiating from my heated loins as Miss Suzanne performed the same tribute on me. I could feel I was close to a powerful climax. My hips were moving involuntarily, as if I were fucking, to use the colloquially naughty term.

Above me, Lady Anna was obviously at the height of ecstatic pleasure. The sweetly pungent juices seemed to pour from her depths, soaking my face, filling my mouth, acting as a trigger to my own ecstasy.

Once was not enough for Lady Anna, nor for me. And Miss Suzanne, though dilligent in pleasuring me, had not had her own needs addressed, so we formed a little circle on the bed. I had my head between Miss Suzanne's legs, her ladyship was tonguing my quaking quim, and Miss Suzanne was tonguing her school chum's. It was all very improper, to be sure. I suspected that none of us were that concerned with convention. Oh, my mother would heartily disapprove, but that meant nothing at all, for my mother was safely in Ireland, where she could exert no power over me at all.

When each of us had gained release at least twice more, I redressed in my uniform and took my leave of two very satisfied women. I did not put my corset back on, but rolled it up and carried it under my left arm. Should anyone happen to be about, for all they could tell I was simply taking one of Lady Anna's corsets to repair. It was late, and the halls are never so well-lit that anyone would notice my unfettered figure in passing.

I shall have to remember all that transpired to-night. Perhaps I can make use of it in a future book.

IX: Suzanne Willis's Diary

Thursday, 17th July— I am worried about my darling Anna. Last night, after we had finished with her maid, who proved to be a *marvellous* quim lapper, we fell asleep in each other's arms, as we usually do.

I could hear the clock in the hall striking two when I came suddenly awake. The bed was moving. I rolled over toward Anna, and was very surprised to find her once again in the posture of a woman making love to a man. She was moaning softly in pleasure, and I was shocked to realise that her dear, sweet little cunt was gaping open, moving as if being stretched and pleasured by a huge male member. How in the world, I wondered, was *that* possible?

At her climax, she threw back her head. Those two little marks grew suddenly livid and seemed to grow larger, blood pouring from them, yet somehow simply vanishing. It had to be some sort of strange illusion, I thought.

When she relaxed, and again fell asleep, I cradled her in my arms, sleeping with my head resting upon her shoulder.

It was when we awoke that I noticed the change. Anna has always been vivacious, eager to try new things, to experience everything the world has on offer. This morning, however, she seemed strangely lethargic, as if all her energy had been drained away in the night.

I rang for O'Leary, but was surprised to find Mrs Irving, the housekeeper, entering the room instead. 'Where is O'Leary?' I asked.

'She had to go into the village on a personal matter,' Mrs Irving replied. 'But I presume I can fill in for her?'

'Yes,' I said, 'I am sure that you can. As you can see, Lady Anna is not herself this morning.'

Mrs Irving approached the bed and looked critically at her mistress, who hardly acknowledged her presence. 'Why, so she is, the poor dear. When did this come on?'

'It must have been while she slept,' I answered. 'She was full of energy when we retired for the night. Now she seems to have none at all, and she looks so pale.'

Mrs Irving nodded briskly. 'Well, I shall send a groom with the dog-cart to fetch Doctor Allen. Perhaps he can see something that we cannot. Then I shall return and help you dress.' She looked at both of us. 'And, I think, if the doctor will be here, we must see that her ladyship is wearing a proper night dress, don't you think?'

Only then did I realise that Anna and I were both still quite naked.

'Yes,' I said. 'That would certainly be a good idea. It was a very hot night, you see.'

Mrs Irving could say more with an arched eyebrow than most could say in a thousand-word essay. Still, I think her only real concern was Anna. She hurried away to despatch the groom and dog-cart, and I climbed out of bed and started to dress. I was nearly finished by the time Mrs Irving returned.

X: Doctor Allen's Journal

17th July, 11 o'clock AM— I have just examined Lady Anna Corwin. I find I am at somewhat of a loss to explain her condition. She has been my patient for the last five years, ever since I took over the practice from Doctor Wallace. During that time, I have not found reason to treat her for anything more serious than a sprained wrist sustained in a fall from a horse. Beyond that, I merely performed her annual health check, which never revealed any problems at all.

When I arrived at the New Lodge, after being summoned by a groom, who also collected me in a dog-cart and drove me to the house, I initially encountered Lord Muntglare. He had been informed of his sister's sudden illness, and conducted me to her room, which she shared with Miss Suzanne Willis, who was introduced to me as a school friend of her ladyship. Miss Willis was kind enough to stay with us during my examination of the patient.

There was nothing obviously wrong with Lady Anna, other than two tiny puncture marks on her throat. I asked Miss Willis, who was evidently sharing the same bed with Lady Anna during her visit, if she had noticed any problems with bed-bugs or other parasites, and she assured me that she had found no evidence of such a thing. If these were insect bites, presumably they happened out of doors, and not in the bedroom.

Still, she was rather lethargic, and rather paler than I liked. I wondered if she might be suffering from some form of anaemia, though the sudden onset of the condition seemed to rule against that. On the other hand, my sphygmomanometer revealed a blood pressure of only 100 millimetres[1], which is quite low. Was it possible blood was not deficient, but actually missing? I didn't see how that was possible. There was no abdominal distension, as you would expect if she were bleeding internally, and whilst she did exhibit those two wounds, there was no blood on the bedclothes, which there surely would have been had she bled enough to cause this condition during the night.

I was quite at a loss to explain what was wrong with her.

I said as much to Lord Muntglare, suggesting that the best thing for her would likely be a good, solid meal. His Lordship said he would, of course, arrange that. I also suggested that I might wish to consult my old teacher, Sir Ulrich Heilger, who had considerable experience with obscure conditions. His Lordship encouraged me to do so, and to arrange for a consultation at the earliest possible time.

---

1   In 1895, blood pressure measurement was still a fairly recent development, and only systolic readings were being taken. It would be a few more years before it occurred to anyone that measuring diastolic pressure would also be useful, or, possibly, before anyone realised that this was possible.

XI: Letter, Doctor Allen to Doctor Heilger

17th July, 1895
Dudley House, High Coulston

My Dear Sir Ulrich:

I have the honour of presenting you with a most unusual case. The patient is a 22-year-old woman of noble birth, and who previously has been in the best of health. She awakened this morning apparently exhausted and too weak to get out of bed. I was summoned, but could find nothing obviously wrong with her, beyond a surprisingly low blood pressure reading of 100, and a depressed temperature of only 96.8 degrees. She is also quite wan.

I should greatly appreciate it if you were able to come to High Coulston and conduct your own examination at your earliest convenience. The patient's noble brother has assured me that he would welcome your consultation, as he is quite concerned with his sister's health.

I remain, as ever,

Sincerely,

GEORGE ALLEN, MB BS

XII: Letter, Doctor Heilger to Doctor Allen

18th July
St. Bartholomew's Hospital, London

My Dear Friend:

I have just this moment received your letter, and I shall, of course, be delighted to consult with you on your case. I am unable to come up to High Coulston to-day, having a very serious operation scheduled for this after-noon, but shall arrive on the 10 o'clock train to-morrow. I look forward to seeing you, and seeing what has become of a favourite student.

I am,

Yours sincerely,
ULRICH HEILGER, KCB, DPhil, MD, FRS

XIII: Lady Anna Corwin's Journal

Thursday, 18th July— No journal yesterday. I was quite exhausted, and could hardly muster the energy to climb out of bed and totter to the loo. It was rather embarrassing to have to have my darling Suzanne help me with that most intimate function. True, this was by no means the first time she has seen me make water, or even helped me to do so, but on all previous occasions this was not because of any physical weakness on my part, but out of a more personal, sensuous motive.

The doctor came in the morning and examined me. I explained that I had no idea of what was wrong. I had that same odd dream of a nocturnal visit from Lord Ravensbrook, but did not see any reason to mention this to the doctor. He is seeking physical clues, not metaphysical ones. In any event, it was just a dream, and cannot possibly have caused my problem. Suzanne tells me she again observed my dreaming state, and that, though physically I seemed to be engaged in sexual intercourse, there was no one there.

The doctor's prescription was little more than to eat and drink and so build up my strength. The entire household seemed intent on seeing that this edict was carried out. All during the day, I was visited by Mrs Irving, my brother, Suzanne, and O'Leary, all bringing hot tea, or little biscuits or cakes. This in addition to the wonderful beef roast served at supper. I fear I may have eaten too much in pursuit of restored health, and shall have to be careful or I may find my clothing has grown smaller during my illness.

Last night, I slept cradled in Suzanne's arms. I did not dream last night, or, if I did, I do not remember. I awoke much refreshed. True, I was still rather tired, but nothing at all like the previous day, when I could hardly move. I was energetic enough to insist that Suzanne allow me to lick her precious quim as a way of thanking her for her help yesterday. I did not have to expend too much effort encouraging her, and she eagerly reciprocated, making me climax twice. Oh, I do feel *so* much better.

Doctor Allen came by close to tea time. He seemed happy to find me more my old self. Still, he informed me, he had called in a specialist, who would arrive on the morning train to-morrow to consult. I told him that I hoped I should be fine by then, but would certainly be willing to speak with his friend. I was not fully recovered, after all, and who knew when this strange lethargy might strike again?

XIV: Lord Muntglare's Journal

Tuesday, 18th July — I was tied up with estate business much of the morning, though I did find time to look in upon my dear sister. She was dressed, and sitting by the window of her room, chatting with Miss Willis, when I entered. In answer to my query anent her health, she responded:

'I feel much better. I cannot imagine why I was so weak yesterday, but the good food and drink, and a peaceful night's rest, have done wonders.'

'Do let me know if there is anything you need,' I told her. 'Anything at all.'

Her smile was perhaps not so dazzling as it normally is, but she seemed much more her old self for all that. 'I believe I shall be fine, Neddy,' she replied.

I turned my attention to Miss Willis. 'I have estate business that will occupy me most of the morning,' I said, 'but I plan to take a long walk about the estate after luncheon. It would be most agreeable if you could join me, Miss Willis. It will give you a further opportunity to view the grounds, and, perhaps, we shall become better acquainted in the process.'

Miss Willis is, as I have remarked previously in this journal, a most attractive young woman.

'I should like that very much, your lordship,' she responded.

'Excellent. I should think about half one would be an excellent time to start.'

'I will be ready.'

I finished my work in good time, and we all enjoyed a fine luncheon meal, served at the very stroke of noon. By half one I had changed into tweeds, better suited for rambling over the estate than the morning suit I had been wearing, and met Miss Willis in the front parlour.

She was, likewise, dressed for activity, wearing a white shirtwaist under a grey waistcoat, and a rather full grey shirt that I thought would allow her an easy gait. All I could see of her foot gear were the tips, but her boots or shoes appeared to be rather thick-soled, so I presume they had been chosen for comfortable walking and not for style. Her straw hat had a wide brim, and was held on by a pink ribbon fastened beneath her pretty chin.

'Are you ready?' I asked.

'I am, your lordship.'

'Call me Edwin when we are alone,' I suggested. I thought of suggesting 'Neddy,' which had always been Anna's pet name for me, but decided we should become just a bit better acquainted before allowing that degree of familiarity.

'And you may call me Suzanne,' she said.

'I should like that.'

We walked out through the kitchen door. There is a gravel path that runs through the estate, making a circuit that takes the stroller down the main drive, along the low wall that runs by the road, and through the woods bordering Lord Ravensbrook's new estate, along Fortman's Brook, around the lake, and back to the Old House. From there, of course, it is a matter of only a few minutes' walk to return to the New Lodge, perhaps stopping in the stables on the way to admire the magnificent animals that are kept there.

'My sister seems much improved to-day,' I said, as we reached the end of the drive and took the path along the wall.

'She does, indeed,' Suzanne replied. 'I held her all night, and perhaps that may have helped. She was terribly active in her sleep the night before, when the troubles started.'

'Active in what way?' I asked.

'Moving in the bed. It was almost as if she were fighting with someone.'

'Fighting? I trust she didn't hit you.'

'No, no, nothing of the sort. It was just that her limbs were in constant motion. It was all very strange. And, in retrospect, I can see how it might have exhausted her, for if she was sleeping during all of this, she was still using a great deal of energy.'

'Did you mention this to Doctor Allen?'

'Lady Anna did. I merely confirmed it.'

We walked in silence for a few minutes. Looking over the wall, I noticed a sombre, black hearse coming along the road towards the village. Calling over the wall, I stopped Mr. Zelling, for it was the undertaker himself who was driving the single black horse drawing the vehicle. 'What brings you out this way, Mr. Zelling?' I asked.

'Sad news, your lordship,' Zelling replied. He gestured behind him, where a simple oaken coffin could be seen through the glass panels of the hearse. 'I was, unfortunately, about the business of retrieving Miss Naomi Cooper and conveying her back to my establishment.'

'Miss Cooper?' I gasped. 'Why, she's only a child.'

'Eighteen, six weeks ago, her mother told me, sir.'

'What happened to her?' I presumed some sort of accident. The Coopers' farm was located half a mile beyond Lord Ravensbrook's drive. They kept a few Friesian cows, some pigs, some sheep, and raised two or three varieties of corn. Wheat, certainly, and perhaps oats or barley, or perhaps both. Farms could be dangerous. One could fall from a height, be savaged by a sow, fall off a horse, or in front of a plough.

'That's the strangest thing, your lordship,' Zelling said. 'It seems she simply died. She'd been feeling poorly for a day of so, but had been improving, and then, last night, she went to bed and simply failed to wake up this morning. Her mother found her dead in her bed, poor thing.' He shook his head. 'I fear the police will insist Doctor Allen perform a post mortem, which is sure to be upsetting to her family, to say nothing of delaying the funeral.'

'The Vicar will not be happy about that,' I commented. I turned to Suzanne. 'Our vicar is a crusty old soul who was once a colonel of grenadiers before taking the cloth. I'm afraid he often still acts the martinet.'

'I'd best be along, your lordship,' Zelling said. 'If they decide there must be a post mortem, best to get on with it as quickly as possible and minimise the delay.'

I nodded, and Zelling snapped the reins against the horse's back. The animal snorted and resume trotting along the road towards the village.

Suzanne looked at me with genuine concern. She would naturally feel sympathy for the poor dead girl, but I knew that wasn't all. She was certainly thinking about Anna. The Cooper girl had been feeling poorly, started to improve, and then suddenly died in the night. Could it be that they both suffered from the same malady? The similarity was obvious, though I am sure we both naturally hoped that the outcome would be different.

We continued with our walk, soon coming to the end of the roadside path and turning back into the estate. Suzanne was the first to voice concern.

'Is it possible,' she said, in a nervous tone, 'that whatever malady is affecting your dear sister may be the same that struck down the young woman in the hearse? I cannot help but fear, for the symptoms seem so like.'

'I think it unlikely,' I said. 'Is there a connexion between the two? My sister hardly travels in the same circles as the Cooper girl.'

'Might they not have encountered each other in the village? At church, perhaps?'

'I suppose that is possible,' I admitted. 'Or in the book shop, where the girl was employed, if memory serves. Still, I think it unlikely we are dealing with anything contagious. After all, you have shared my sister's bed for the last fortnight, and only she has fallen ill. If it were easily spread, should you not also be afflicted?'

Suzanne walked silently beside me for a time. I suppose she was thinking about what I had said. After what happened in my studio the day after her arrival, I had little doubt that their sharing of a bed entailed a most intimate familiarity. Only one was ill, therefore it could not be something easily transmitted.

We soon entered the woods. Here it was possible to imagine what this country had been like in ancient times. These trees were hundreds of years old. There is one great oak that I have no doubt was already well grown when the Lion Heart sat upon the throne. The path goes by this forest giant, which is nearly a hundred feet high, and spreads nearly as wide.

'I can imagine Robin Hood taking shelter here,' I remarked. 'Or, I could, if this were Sherwood.'

Suzanne smiled at this. 'I fear we are a good, long way from Nottingham, Edwin. Is there not some local outlaw who might take good Locksley's place?'

'Only a highwayman called Black Morris,' I said. 'But he never gathered any followers, and wasn't at all the romantic paragon. No, he proved to be the smith's son, from Hawthorn Croft, and by the time he was caught and hanged he'd murdered a dozen men and ravished nearly as many women whilst committing his depredations on the high road. Just an ugly, evil-hearted lout, and dead now nearly a century.'

'Your sister confided in me that she carried a revolver when they drove to the station to collect me,' Suzanne said. 'Is there still a risk?'

I shook my head. 'No, I don't believe there is. Precautions are always in order, naturally, but there have been no robberies on the local roads in many years.'

Suzanne was cautiously exploring the area under the great oak. The foliage was so dense that grass would not grow, but the ground was thickly covered in fallen leaves.

A great stag ventured into the clear area beneath the oak. Both of us froze in place, watching him. Then a brief puff of wind carried our scent to him. He snorted and bolted back into the forest. I couldn't help but wonder how an animal with that magnificent set of antlers could move so swiftly in the dense wood.

'I almost feel like throwing off my garments and acting the primitive in this sylvan setting,' Suzanne remarked.

'I wouldn't object,' I said. 'I'd only regret that I did not bring a camera to capture such a lovely sight.'

'Would you do that?'

I nodded. 'Naturally. You have a beautiful body, and this is a lovely setting. You could let your hair down, and objectify the woodland nymph of legend.'

She smiled. 'Perhaps,' she said, 'before I return home, you may bring me out here again, *with* your camera, and we may do what you suggest. You are a wonderful photographer, and the images you took of me, and of Anna, were quite beautiful.'

'I am very happy you liked them. It was a great pleasure taking them.'

'You have been very kind to me, Edwin, allowing me to stay in your home.'

'It is my sister's home as much as mine,' I noted. 'At least, until she marries. You are *her* guest, really, but I find I enjoy your company very much, so, even if you did not know her, I should always be happy to accommodate you here.'

'Still, I feel I should do something to show my gratitude.'

'Your company is compensation enough.'

Suzanne moved close, putting an arm around me and pressing her body against mine. 'I was thinking, dear Edwin, that you might again reveal that magnificent endowment, and allow me to worship briefly at the altar of your masculinity.'

I wasn't quite sure what to say. Naturally, the first thought that entered my mind was to scream, 'Yes, please.' I managed not to blurt that out.

Suzanne was taking the question out of my hands. She knelt in front of me and began to unbutton my trouser fly. It seemed the gentlemanly thing to do to permit this lovely young lady to fulfil whatever desire might have taken possession of her.

In a trice, she had opened my fly, reached in, and extracted my generative organ. Whilst I am forced to admit that, if only from surprise, it was nothing much to look at when first she brought it out into the dappled light under the great oak, her mere touch was sufficient for it to quickly begin to grow and harden.

Her soft hands gently stroked the turgid staff. She leaned close, rubbing the purple knob against her cheek and sighing prettily. I will admit to having a particular weakness for red hair, and as I looked down at her coppery coif, at my manhood pressed against her lovely face, those bright green eyes looking up at me, I felt an erotic impulse that would not be denied.

Suzanne gently kissed the tip of my rampant manhood. Her sweet lips opened, taking the shaft between them, her lips sliding up and down along each side of the steely rod in turn, her pink tongue darting out, circling the knob, her mouth opening and engulfing me. My hips were moving involuntarily, thrusting my throbbing organ into her hot mouth.

When I could stand it no longer, she suddenly withdrew her mouth and released my trembling spear, which glistened with her saliva. She stood up, bent over, leaning her hands against the great oak, and with one hand pulled her dress and petticoats up over her beautiful arse. 'Drive that big log into me,' she demanded. 'Thrill me, fill me.'

I got behind her and started to press myself against her dear quim, but she stopped me, saying, 'Not there, dear Edwin. Put it in my bum. We mustn't take any chances, though I should dearly love to.'

Still slick from her enthusiastic oral ministrations, I pressed my rock-hard shaft against her rosy portal. It went in with only a little effort. Never before have I felt anything so hot or so tight. She was moaning with passion as I drove my manhood in and out of her behind. Her fingers were working in her fragrant cunt, and soon she was crying out in her passion, her slender body convulsing with pleasure.

I could hold out no longer. My manhood began to pulse, filling her bum with what felt like months of pent-up spunk, throbbing, driving, blasting my essence deep inside her.

When I had withdrawn, and Suzanne had come down from her climax and was standing there, her costume restored to order, looking as if nothing at all untoward had happened, I was seized with an uncontrollable impulse to hold her tightly to me.

'You are a wonderful, wonderful girl,' I told her.

She smiled wistfully. 'That was quite lovely,' she said. 'Tis a pity it must be only a fleeting *affaire de Cœur.*'

'Why must it be so?' I asked.

'We must consider our stations, dear Edwin. You are an earl, and I am the daughter of a barrister. We do not live in the same circles, and I am here only because I once shared a room at school with your darling sister. Had I not known her, I cannot imagine we should ever have met at all.'

I was touched by the nobility of spirit expressed in these words. Even though a union betwixt the two of us would certainly be possible, we were, indeed, of vastly different social classes. One would like to believe that these artificial strata mean little when it comes to anything touching upon *l'amour,* but society is unwilling to agree. By these words, dear Suzanne was telling me that I should not feel obligated towards her; should not permit my chivalrous senses to compel any action that society might not countenance.

Indeed, the very manner of her love-making, of having me take her in her bum, and not in a more appropriate place, seemed now a part of this. There could be no chances taken that some accident might place me under any compulsion towards her.

I kissed her tenderly upon the forehead. 'Come,' I said, 'we should continue our walk. Anna will be expecting us to return, and who knows how she is feeling by now. Perhaps she will be fully recovered.'

And so we set off, back towards the New Lodge, walking hand in hand until we emerged from the woods and into the open grounds, where someone might see us and draw some unwarranted—well, perhaps fully warranted, but still potentially scandalous—conclusion.

XV: Clipping from the High Coulston *Record*

UNUSUAL DEATH OF A YOUNG LADY

19th July— The village was shocked to learn of the untimely death of Miss Naomi Cooper, of the Cooper Farm, Morristown Road, sometime during the night of 17th–18th July. The unfortunate young woman was discovered by her mother shortly after 7 o'clock of that morning, when she failed to emerge from her room at the usual time to depart for her employment at Elliott's Book Shop on the High Street.

According to Mr. Elliott, 'Naomi was an excellent employee, and very popular with our patrons. Quite well-read, and always ready to offer suggestions as to books that a customer might find suitable. She will be missed.'

Mr. Josiah Cooper, the girl's father, was recently the winner of High Coulston's annual 'Model Farm' award, and is well known in the local agricultural community. He was unable to enlighten this reporter as to any unusual circumstances surrounding the death of his daughter. 'She'd been feeling poorly,' he informed us, 'but afore she retired the night before she'd been much better, smiling and laughing, very like her old self. Then, in the morning, my wife found her dead. I cannot understand any of this, but, I doubt it's for us to understand, is it? God will do what God will do.'

Mrs Cooper has secluded herself, and was unwilling to speak to this reporter. One can certainly understand her reluctance, for it must have been a great shock to discover her only child dead in her bed for no apparent reason.

As there had been no previous indication of any serious illness, Inspector Royce, of the County Constabulary, upon consultation with the Coroner, Mr. Williard, requested that a post-mortem examination be conducted. This was performed by Doctor Allen. Whilst the results have not been officially released, pending the Coroner's Inquest, this reporter has learned that, other than an unusual anaemia, there was no indication of any obvious health issues, nor any indication that the death was in any way unnatural.

The unfortunate young lady will be laid to rest in Saint Wilfred's churchyard on Saturday at 10 o'clock, the Reverend Ogilvy officiating. The family will receive friends this evening in the reception parlour of Mr. Zelling's undertaking establishment, No. 14, Swallow Lane.

XVI: Doctor Allen's Journal

Friday, 19th July— As promised, Sir Ulrich arrived on the ten o'clock train. I collected him in my gig, and apprised him of more details during the short ride to my surgery. He would stay in High Coulston for as long as it seemed likely he could be useful, or until the patient succumbed. Naturally, we both hoped the latter would not come to pass. Not for many years, at least.

'You had a death from a similar complaint, I understand?' Sir Ulrich prompted.

'Yes,' I replied. 'Miss Naomi Cooper. She was an 18-year-old shop girl, still living on her parents' farm. I have been in the book shop where she was employed many times, and found her a gentle, soft-spoken, and very beautiful young woman. I did not treat her during her illness, which her father informs me was brief, but, as she had been a healthy young woman, and died so suddenly, I was called in by Mr. Williard, the coroner, and asked to perform a post mortem.'

'What did you find?'

'Only an extreme anaemia,' I replied. 'Everything else was entirely normal. All of her organs were healthy. She was still *virgo intacto*, which one would expect, for she comes from a very strict family. It appeared death was caused by a loss of blood, yet there was no bleeding, neither internal nor external, that I could discern. She appeared to have lost enough that her bedding should have been soaked in blood, yet her father assures me this was not the case.'

Sir Ulrich looked thoughtful. After a very long pause, he asked, 'What is to be done with her?'

'I have released her body to the undertaker. She will be buried to-morrow, in the local churchyard.'

Sir Ulrich nodded. 'I see.'

We arrived at my surgery and I helped Sir Ulrich carry his bags up to the guest room in my quarters, which are located above. He took a few minutes to freshen up, then joined me in a light lunch, served by my faithful house-keeper, Mrs Dumphy.

After lunch, we drove out to Muntglare. I was pleased to discover that Lady Anna was much improved from when I had examined her two days previously. She was up and about, and we were able to see her in the front parlour, where she was joined by her brother, that is, Lord Muntglare, and her friend, Miss Willis.

As usual, the introduction of Sir Ulrich, with his impressive collection of post nominals, was greeted with a bit of awe. It's not every day that one is introduced to a distinguished physician who not only holds doctoral degrees in both medicine and philosophy, but has also been invested Knight Commander of the Bath.

Lady Anna spoke brightly about current events in the village, and seemed especially curious about the late Miss Cooper. 'I suppose I shall have to attend the funeral,' she said. 'I believe their farm is rented from us, is it not, Neddy?'

'Until quite recently, yes. Father was able to arrange for them to purchase the land outright shortly before he passed.' Lord Muntglare turned to Sir Ulrich and me. 'It was a very complicated undertaking,' he said, 'for it involved breaking the tail on those eighteen acres the Coopers had been farming as tenants for, I suppose, the past two or three centuries. Father felt that the land should be theirs, as they had occupied it for so long.'

Sir Ulrich, who despite his thoroughly British titles, is still, at heart, a bit of a Prussian, enquired, 'Is that a good idea, your lordship? By breaking the tail, surely he was diminishing your patrimony.'

'In all honesty, Sir Ulrich, he did not, as the funds were set aside to pay the death duties on the estate. My father, you see, was quite aware that he would soon fall victim to an insidious complaint. He was, to his way of thinking, providing for a smooth passage of the estate without forcing upon me an onerous tax debt, which would no doubt have compelled the sale of other assets in any case. He did me, and my sister, a great favour. The Cooper farm was not, in any event, contiguous to the rest of the estate, the intervening land having long ago passed out of our possession.'

Sir Ulrich nodded his comprehension. 'Now, however, I think it best if Doctor Allen and I examine her ladyship. She appears well to-day, but one must always be wary of a relapse.'

'Of course,' Lord Muntglare replied, nodding.

'If your ladyship has no objection,' Sir Ulrich said, 'might we retire to your boudoir? I doubt the parlour is an appropriate locale for what may, of necessity, be a rather intimate examination, if you'll pardon my saying so.'

'Of course,' Lady Anna replied, rising.

'Miss Willis may, of course, accompany us,' I suggested.

'Naturally,' Sir Ulrich agreed.

Sir Ulrich and I followed Lady Anna and Miss Willis out of the parlour, up the main staircase, and down a dimly-lit corridor to Lady Anna's bedchamber. This had seemed rather a gloomy place when I was here two days ago, but now the draperies had been thrown open, and the room was flooded with sunlight, turning it into a bright, pleasant retreat.

'I am afraid I must ask you to remove your stays,' Sir Ulrich said to Lady Anna. 'If it will not prove too distressing, it would be best were you to wear only a night dress.'

'Whatever you wish, Sir Ulrich.'

'Doctor Allen and I will step out into the corridor. You may call us back in when you are ready, Lady Anna.'

It was some ten minutes by my watch when Miss Willis opened the door and asked us to return. Lady Anna had removed her clothing and slipped on a cotton night dress, and was now lying in her bed, with a sheet pulled up under her chin.

Sir Ulrich conducted a standard examination. He employed a stethoscope to auscultate her heart, lungs, and viscera. Donning a head mirror, he had Lady Anna take a seat in front of a window, where he could conveniently examine her ears and throat using the reflected sunlight for illumination. I found myself perforce looking away, for the sunlight streaming through the window shone through the thin cotton, silhouetting the patient's beautifully-proportioned body, and outlining her perfect bosom.

I looked back, after Lady Anna had returned to the bed and again covered herself. Sir Ulrich was seated on a chair beside the bed, leaning over her closely, examining her neck with a small hand glass.

'Do you know where these marks come from?' he asked her.

Lady Anna shook her head. 'I do not,' she replied. 'I woke up with them Saturday last. The windows are left open while we sleep on these hot nights, so I suppose some insect may have come in during the night and caused them.'

'We?'

'Suzanne sleeps in here with me,' Lady Anna told him. 'We were dear friends at school, and her sharing my bed allows us to talk late into the night ere we fall asleep.'

Sir Ulrich nodded, understandingly. 'Ah,' he said, 'the dear comfort of long friendship. But, you did not actually notice anything during the night.'

'No, nothing.'

Here, he looked at Miss Willis, who nodded agreement.

Sir Ulrich sat there in thought for some minutes. At length, he spoke: 'I have an idea, but, for now, it is hardly formed, and I very much doubt that it is true in any event. However, this is what I would ask you to do. Warm as it is this time of year, I think it best if you sleep with the windows closed. I am also going to suggest that, before you sleep, you make for yourself a garland of garlic, and sleep with this about your neck.'

'Garlic?' Lady Anna exclaimed. 'What will this do?'

'Garlic has surprisingly salutary properties,' Sir Ulrich answered. 'And biting things find it repulsive, so it may save you from further troubles. You seem healthy now, but so did Miss Cooper, from what Doctor Allen has told me, just before her unfortunate death. I would prefer not to take chances.

'I have heard of similar cases to yours on the Continent, but I shall have to travel to Berlin to investigate further. While I am gone, I suggest the garlic.' He reached into his pocket and produced a small silver cross on a silver chain. 'And, for luck, I suppose you could say, I would like you to wear this about your neck as well. It has been blessed by the Bishop of London.'

'Church of England, I presume, Sir Ulrich?' Lady Anna asked.

'Naturally.'

'Then I shall wear it gladly,' she said, taking the offered cross and chain, and fastening it around her neck.'

Sir Ulrich rose from his chair. 'Then I shall return in a few days, dear lady. I hope to find that you are fully recovered when I do.'

We took our leave of the ladies. Lord Muntglare met us at the foot of the stairs. We told him what we could, which I fear was less than he wished to know. We simply did not have a definitive diagnosis as yet. Sir Ulrich clearly suspected something, having left his strange instructions, but I was at a loss to imagine just what it was.

'What do you suspect?' I asked, as we drove back to my surgery.

Sir Ulrich looked at me with a very serious expression upon his craggy face. 'Something one can only describe as fantastical,' he replied. 'But, I am not certain. The signs appear to be there, yet there may be some other explanation. No, I must consult, and that means a journey to Berlin. When is the next train for London?'

I pulled out my watch. 'I fear you have just missed it,' I reported. 'The next will not be until nine o'clock this evening.'

'I must be on it.' He looked thoughtful. 'I do not suppose it is possible to engage a special in this little village.'

'Not easily. Very likely,' I told him, 'it would take just as long or longer than waiting for the next regular train, as I believe the railroad would have to bring the locomotive and car from Leicester, or possibly from farther away, should there be none available there.'

'Very well. I shall sup with you, then catch the nine o'clock train and make my arrangements to travel to Berlin.' He thought a moment more. 'I do not suppose there is a direct train from here to Harwich? It would save some time, as I will have to take the ferry from there to Rotterdam.'

I shook my head. 'Not that I am aware of.'

Nor was there, when we enquired at the station. Sir Ulrich would have to travel first to London, then on to Harwich, take a ferry to Rotterdam, and resume travelling by rail from there to Berlin. He estimated that he would be gone for at least a week, between travelling and consulting with his informant. He would not tell me what he suspected, other than to stress the importance of the garlic garland and cross when Lady Anna was sleeping. Both, he said, would serve to ward off a worsening of her illness, though, for the life of me, the only thing I could imagine they would ward off were other people. We English are not partial to pungent herbs.

XVII: Suzanne Willis's Diary

Friday, 19 July — The physicians have come and gone, and we are none the wiser when it comes to darling Anna's ailment. Doctor Allen is a pleasant, good-looking young bachelor, I should say in his early thirties, with thick, wavy blond hair and the bluest eyes I have ever seen. The consultant, Sir Ulrich Heilger, is much older, perhaps in his middle-sixties, with thinning grey hair, and cold, grey eyes. There is something very formal about him. I understand, though he is now a British subject and, indeed, a knight commander of the Most Honourable Order of the Bath, that he is, by birth, a Prussian. That would certainly explain the formality and stern attitude. He is also very learned, being both a doctor of medicine and a doctor of philosophy.

Yet he has left the most unusual orders. Anna is to wear a wreath of garlic about her pretty throat when she retires to sleep, and to keep a little silver cross always about her neck. Whatever can these things mean?

After the doctors departed, we remained in our room for some time. Anna quickly discarded her night dress, lounging upon the bed, turned towards me, resting her pretty head upon her left hand whilst the right roamed sensuously over her beautiful form.

'Feeling better?' I asked.

She smiled seductively. 'Much. Come and join me.'

How could I refuse? I rose from my chair and walked to the bed. Rather than waste time with laces and whalebone, I simply removed my skirt, petticoats, and pantalets, threw off my shirtwaist, and climbed into bed with stays and bodice in place.

Anna lay back, laughing. I knelt between her drawn-up legs, leaned forward, and spread her nether lips with my fingers. I bent closer, inhaling the musky sweet scent. My tongue extended, swirled around her glistening pink pearl of pleasure, delved between her lips to taste the sweet nectar of her passion.

I could lap up my darling Anna's juices forever, revelling in the way her strong, lithe body reacts to the adoration. One sees those great religious monuments to certain lady saints, and, if one knows someone as uninhibited, as free, as my darling, one knows that religious ecstasy is nothing more than the purely physical ecstasy a woman can rise to when a loving tongue lifts her to the very heights of carnal pleasure.

Yet my darling has other ideas. Now we both lie on the bed, facing away from each other, our legs twined around each other's bodies, the kinky red hair adorning my mount pressed against and mingling with Anna's golden thatch as we press out private parts together in a primitive carnal rhythm. Anna begins to cry out in her ecstasy, reaching the first of many climaxes much more quickly than I, for she has the advantage of a considerable start while I was serving her.

I am not far behind. Every nerve in my body is crying out with the intensity of my pleasure. I do love my darling so. I want her to be forever young and filled with joy, and I want to share her bed, let our bodies join together in ecstatic orgies of sensuality.

As we lay together in the aftermath, my darling Anna's fingers toying with my hard nipples, her gentle lips kissing my shoulder, I felt satisfied, yet with an underlying recognition of potential sorrow to come. One day, perhaps not too distant a day, each of us would marry. Our current joyous couplings would cease, and there would only be the more brutal carnality of the marriage bed.

'We should never marry,' I said, my voice sad.

'Will we have a choice in that?' Anna wondered. 'I have several suitors, though none seem too ardent. I fear they see me more as a prize than as a potential partner.'

'If there were only some way a woman could marry, yet remain mistress of her own destiny. I have only a little money, but the day will come when I inherit my mother's house, which is of some little value, and, if I am married at that time, or marry after, of what use is an inheritance that immediately becomes my husband's property? Why should I not keep what is mine, just as any husband will retain what is his?'

'My brother is being courted by three or four American heiresses,' Anna said. 'Or, perhaps, I should say, he is being courted by their mothers on their behalf. We own a great deal of land, but it does not bring in nearly so much money as this estate requires. Any of the American women would bring with her vast amounts of money.'

'Your brother,' I said, 'has a lovely generative organ.' There was no harm in saying this, for she knew I had seen it in Edwin's photographic studio, and felt his hot spunk upon my back. I did not think I needed to mention I had a more recent, even more intimate acquaintanceship with that beautiful staff.

'He does, at that,' Anna agreed. 'And a wonderfully wicked way about him. Something I fear will be lost, should he marry one of those heiresses. The spirits of

Cromwell and Calvin find a welcoming home in America, it seems.'

'For now,' I said, 'let us pass the rest of the afternoon napping in each other's arms. We cannot tell what the future will bring, but we can certainly make the most of the present.'

XVIII: Doctor Heilger's *Tagebuch*

Saturday, July 20, on the train— It appears I will have the compartment to myself between Rotterdam and Utrecht, so I will take advantage of the privacy to write up my notes. The patient, Lady A——, is a high-born lady of 22 years, five feet four inches in height, weighing 108 pounds, slender, and has been in excellent health until recently. Doctor Allen was called in on 17th July, at which time the patient was too weak to get out of bed without assistance. When I saw her, on 19th July, she appeared much recovered, was out of bed, dressed, and carrying on with her life in a normal way.

I was informed that another young woman, a Miss C——, had exhibited remarkably similar symptoms, including seeming to recover from her illness, but suddenly died in the night. Doctor Allen performed a post mortem on Miss C——, but found nothing remarkable, save for an extreme anaemia presenting as a literal profound reduction of blood volume.

Examination of Lady A—— disclosed no obvious abnormalities. However, I noted that there were two small wounds upon the patient's throat, over the left external carotid artery. I am much concerned about these wounds, as the patient is unable to remember how they were inflicted. She suspects an insect, but a close examination with my glass leads to the terrible suspicion that they were inflicted by human teeth, and specifically by the upper canine teeth of an adult human male.

I have read of these things, but never before have I observed them in a patient. This appears to me to be the result of a vampiric attack. My common sense rebels at this suspicion. In this modern world, one should not suspect vampires, or even believe that they exist other than as primitive folk lore. The vampire is a creature of Balkan myth. He haunts the superstitious Greek peasant, the simple-minded Carpathian villager, the heathen Oriental, but not a young, modern English noble family.

Still, I have taken precautions. Lady A—— has been instructed to keep her windows closed at night, and to wear both a wreath of garlic and a silver cross about her neck while she sleeps. It is well known that the vampire can abide neither.

Meanwhile, I am on my way to Berlin, where I shall consult with my esteemed colleague, the Herr Professor Ottomar von Elbing, of the university medical faculty. He is an expert on all things obscure, and a noted metaphysician. If anyone knows, it will be he.

XIX: Lady Anna Corwin's Journal

Saturday, 20th July— A restless night. Perhaps it was the garlic. Sir Ulrich insisted that this would be beneficial, but it is uncomfortable and unpleasant. Again, there was that strange dream of the room filling with mist, and of Lord Ravensbrook standing over the bed. Yet, this time, he did not come closer. He merely stood beside my bed, gazing down upon me with a reproachful look, as if I had done something to displease him.

We rose early, dressing for the Cooper girl's funeral. Due to the solemnity of the occasion, Jackson had brought out the Berlin coach, drawn by Zerubbabel and Melchior, both pure black Friesian stallions, and magnificent animals.

Though she did not ride to the funeral with us, I noticed O'Leary, standing with a pretty girl in a plain, black dress, amidst the crowd of villagers. They were standing near Doctor Allen and the estate agent, Mr. Morton, so I wondered if this was her friend, Kathleen. I would have to ask her, once we returned home. It would be useful to attach a face to the name, for O'Leary often mentioned her friend. Her presence here also made me wonder if, perhaps, she had been acquainted with the late Miss Cooper.

Reverend Ogilvy seemed to drone on interminably. He is, perhaps, the most boring clergyman I have ever had the misfortune to know. A very tall man, he often seems so lightly built that you might expect a moderate breeze to whisk him clean away, so one must conclude that his physical prowess has been greatly diminished since his younger days as a guardsman. He now gives the impression of a dour, elderly skeleton only lightly covered with flesh.

He droned on about the virtues of the deceased for who knows how long. I was grateful that I had not pinned my watch to my dress, as I might have done on a happier occasion, for it would only have reminded me of how long it was necessary to endure his annoying voice. Then, again, perhaps it would have told me that this torture was shorter than I perceived it to be. When the Reverend Ogilvy was talking, five minutes could seem like an hour.

At last, he began to read the funeral service proper. It would not be too much longer. The oaken coffin was lowered into the grave, the girl's parents threw in the requisite hands-full of earth, the vicar droned the concluding passages, and it was over.

Idly, I noticed that Lord Ravensbrook's coach was drawn up outside the churchyard. The windows were covered by black shades, and I did not see the marquess, who I presumed must be in the coach. I recalled his strange allergy to sunlight, and his comment about having to go about heavily muffled if he had to be about during daylight hours. So, perhaps, he was in the coach. Or, perhaps, he was not, and the coach was there because the elderly coachman was in attendance. I decided I would have to enquire when next I saw the marquess.

As we drove back from the burial, I sat in the rear-facing seat. My brother and dear Suzanne occupied the other. I couldn't avoid noticing that Neddy was constantly glancing over at my friend, or that she would surreptitiously return his glance with a shy smile. I knew they had spent a goodly part of Thursday afternoon walking around the estate. Now I found myself wondering if, perhaps, I should ask Suzanne just what had happened on their walk. Neddy can be such a terrible snob at times, and we certainly need the infusion of cash his marriage to one of his American heiresses would bring, so I must presume that, whatever might be between them, it involved no permanent attachment.

I should like nothing better than for Suzanne to become my sister-in-law. She has exactly that independent spirit, and quick intelligence, that would perfectly complement my brother's usually rather sanguine personality. Still, as she says, she is far from wealthy. If Neddy is leading her on, I fear it will be to no avail. He will undoubtedly settle on one of the Americans, and I fear that he might break poor Suzanne's heart in so doing.

XX: Doctor Heilger's *Tagebuch*

Sunday, 21st July, Berlin— The train having arrived at the Lehrter Bahnhof shortly before one o'clock this morning, I took a cab to the Hotel Kaiserhof, where I had reserved a room. It is the most modern of luxury hotels, and my fourth storey room was easily reached by one of the efficient pneumatic lifts.

The bellman placed my bags on the provided stands, and explained the operation of the electric light, which, I must admit, I found rather harsh and glaring after so many years of living with gas lights, candles, and paraffin lamps. I was very pleased to discover that my room had its own bathroom, and slightly astonished to discover that this was the standard in the *entire* hotel. When I made the reservation, I specified a room with a private bath, but it had hardly occurred to me that *every* room would have that luxury.

I was awakened at eight o'clock in the morning, having left instructions. Making my toilette, I dressed in the proper morning attire, and made my way down to the main lobby, and thence out onto the Wilhelmplatz, where I was able to engage a one-horse cab for the journey to Professor von Elbing's home. The drive took not quite half an hour, and I arrived five minutes early.

The professor is a delightful, white-haired gentleman of eighty-two years. I was surprised at just how short he is. Somehow, I expected a man of his stature to be taller, but he is at least three inches shorter than I, and I lack an inch of being five and a half feet tall.

When we were settled in his study, Professor von Elbing came directly to the point. 'I have read your letter,' he said (we spoke in German), 'and I find it intriguing. Did you actually observe the marks upon your patient's neck?'

'Yes,' I replied. 'They give every appearance of having been made by fangs of some sort.'

'Does your patient remember the attack?'

'She does not appear to. She recalls only waking up with the marks upon her throat, and a feeling of general malaise. Neither she, nor her visiting school friend, who, it appears, shares her bed, recall anything unusual during the night.'

'But this did occur during the night?'

'Yes.'

'That is important,' von Elbing said. 'The vampire's powers are very limited when the sun is in the sky. Almost always, he will retreat to his coffin during those hours, resting against the night, when he emerges to feed upon the blood of the living. Most important of all, when the sun is up, the vampire is trapped in whatever form he had assumed at sunrise.

'For the vampire is a shape-shifter, able to assume the form of the bat, or the wolf, or the rat, or even of an elemental mist, but always reforming at the end into his original human persona. Yet, even as human, he is not limited to the exact form in which he appeared at the time of his death. If the vampire died as an elderly man, and became vampire, he may appear elderly, or he may appear as he did when he was much younger. A vampire who died at the age of eighty, may present himself to the world as a man of twenty.

'As to the length of his un-dead life, no one truly knows. It is said that there are vampires in the world who were once friends of Julius Caesar, or Plato, or Rameses. The vampire may live for thousands of years, if he is not despatched.'

'How do you kill a vampire?' I asked. 'How, for that matter, can you reliably identify him? I should not wish such an accusation to fall upon an innocent, after all.'

The professor rose and walked across the room to a tall book-case. He took a thin, leather-bound volume from a shelf and brought it back to his chair, passing it to me as he resumed his seat. 'You will find everything you need to know in there,' he said.

'*Der Vampir und seine Wege,*' the little book was entitled. '*The Vampire, and His Ways.*' I opened it to a random page and read:

'For that the vampire is a creature lacking a soul, it naturally follows that he fears to be confronted by a mirror, for his reflexion will not appear in the glass. Whenever it is observed that a person does not cast a reflexion in a looking glass, you may be assured that you have encountered one of the un-dead. If you find someone has died unexpectedly, and upon the post mortem table you discover their body has been drained of blood, suspect the vampire is at work. Suspect, and fear, for oft the vampire's victim is, in turn, drawn into this hellish un-dead state, becoming vampire in his turn.'

'I tried to remember what I learned years ago,' I said. 'I have instructed my patient to always wear a wreath of garlic around her neck when she sleeps, and to wear a silver cross about her neck as well.'

Von Elbing nodded gravely. 'Both of those are salutary remedies,' he replied. 'We know not why, yet we do know that the vampire cannot abide garlic. And, naturally, he fears that which is holy. That the cross is silver is, I fear, of little importance. Some will suggest that silver is deadly to the vampire, but most agree that it is not, though it is the one sovereign remedy for the werewolf, who can *only* be killed by silver.'

'What of the vampire?' I asked. 'Is there any remedy, save the stake through the heart?'

'Of course, though the stake is surely the most reliable. And, I must warn you, the stake must be made of wood, and must transfix the vampire at a single stroke. An iron stake will only paralyse him for a brief time, but he will recover, pull it from his breast, and exact his revenge. The same will happen, though it will take longer, if the wooden stake is subject to the hammer more than once as it is driven through his body, so, if you will use the stake, be careful to sharpen it to a needle point, to ensure it will penetrate the heart upon the first hammer blow.

'Exposure to direct sunlight will kill him, for he is so sensitive to sunlight that he will often burst into flames and so perish. Fire will kill him. Cut off his head and he must die. The sexton's shovel is the best implement for this, but a sword will be just as effective. He can only cross running water at the slack tide. A river, or even the merest brook, will bar his passage, unless he be carried across, in a coach, or waggon, or mounted upon a horse, or in his bat form, for it seems this strange inability to pass over running water occurs only close to the stream, not high above it.'

I was writing rapidly in my note-book, wanting to remember everything the Professor said. 'Would that you could come to England with me,' I said. 'Surely, we could make use of your wisdom in our hunt.'

'Alas, that cannot be, my young friend,' von Elbing replied. 'I have lived some eighty-two years now, and my days of clambering over ruined castles are long past.'

I smiled at this. Perhaps more at his referring to me as his 'young' friend than anything else. I am, after all, sixty-four myself, which is hardly young.

'Take the book with you,' he said. 'It may be of help.'

I am writing this on the train to Hanover, thence to Rotterdam via Osnabruck and Utrecht, and the ferry to Harwich. I shall have many hours to read Professor von Ebling's little book, ere I return once again to High Coulston and the task at hand, to find this vampire, and to destroy him.

XXI: Lord Muntglare's Journal

Tuesday, 23rd July— Shortly after three o'clock of the afternoon, as I sat at my desk poring over the monthly ledgers that always remind me, whether I care to admit it or no, that a great estate is not merely a place to live, but a business of sorts, with all the expenses of upkeep, all the responsibilities of collecting rents, or redeeming bond coupons as they become due, of, well, all the myriad little annoyances that serve to vex everyone, from the meanest shop keeper in the village, to an earl of the realm, I heard the sound of a horse and gig coming up the long drive from the road. I went to the window, welcoming any distraction from the ledgers, and found that Doctor Allen was driving his old mare, with Sir Ulrich seated beside him.

A call could only mean that they had news of Anna's illness. She has appeared quite normal, but for a slight weakness, these last few days, yet, naturally, I should wish even that mild discomfort be alleviated.

The two doctors were ushered into my study. After the normal polite preliminaries, and the dispensing of some of my whisky, we gathered in the window corner, with me in my favourite chair, and the two doctors on the settee opposite.

'I have been to Berlin,' Sir Ulrich began. 'Before, I had only suspicion, but now that I have conferred with Profes-

sor von Elbing, I believe I may speak with some authority.'
He took a sip of the whisky, looking at me appraisingly
over the rim of the glass. 'And yet, I fear what I have to say
may not be received favourably, for it is fantastical, and
very much not of the conventional or ordinary.'

'Tell me what you know,' I said. 'This sudden illness
seems so strange as it is, I doubt what you have to say will
be any more shocking.'

'Very well.' He took a slim, leather-bound volume
from his pocket and passed it over to me. I opened it,
then closed it and handed it back to him. My German
comprehension is limited to the odd word that resembles
its English counterpart.

'I fear we are dealing with a vampire,' he said. For a
moment, I feared that Sir Ulrich had of a sudden developed some strange flirtation with humour, but then I
could see that he was serious, and that Doctor Allen was
nodding in agreement.

'A vampire, you say?'

'I fear as much, your lordship.'

'Are we speaking of Polidori's Lord Ruthven? Or of
LeFanu's Countess Karnstein? You cannot be serious, Sir
Ulrich.'

'I felt much the same way at first,' Doctor Allen interjected. 'But now I am convinced. Or, as convinced as I
need to be. Sir Ulrich has learned a great deal from his
visit with Professor von Elbing, and it all makes sense in
this instance.'

'Tell me,' I said.

'It is the nature of the disease, of vampirism, that leads
me in this direction,' Sir Ulrich began. 'At times, when
he is starved of his food, the vampire will kill quickly.
More often, he will find his victim and destroy him — or
her — over a protracted period. If he does not kill at a

stroke, he may prolong his attack over days, or weeks, or even months. He lives on blood, yet he needs only a small amount, so long as he feeds daily.

'Indeed, it is not the loss of blood that kills, except in extreme cases. Perhaps it is as that good Cuban physician, Doctor Finlay, suggests, that something in the vampire's bite brings death, and not the bite itself, as he suspects it is the bite of the mosquito that delivers the contagion of the yellow fever to the poor victim. The victim becomes sick, and rallies, and becomes sick again, in a slow cycle that leads inevitably to death.'

'But, surely,' I said, 'this is only superstition. We are modern men, men who are bang up to date on the latest scientific concepts. Are we to believe in these Balkan legends? Men who are dead, yet not dead? Animated corpses?'

Sir Ulrich rose and began to pace. 'It is as difficult for me, your lordship, as it is for you, to believe these things. I have read of these things, and I remember some tales, told me by my late grand-mother when I was still a child in Potsdam, and it was from these that I prescribed for your beautiful sister. The silver cross, the garlic flowers, these are ancient folk remedies, employed when a vampire was suspected.'

'But why? Why suspect a vampire in the first place? Are such things even heard of in England?'

'You spoke of Polidori before. Now, surely his Count Ruthven was a fictional character, but do you not know that his basis was in reality? I have discovered that in 1798, in our own London, there was an outbreak of vampirism. The truth was kept very quiet, for this had repercussions in some of the highest circles in British society. It was not a count who was implicated, but a royal duke.'

I pondered this revelation. How much credence could I give such an account? Yet, how could I ignore it? My dear sister's life might depend upon my decision to-day.

'But my sister? Why suspect a vampire in her case?'

'Have you not taken note of the marks upon her throat, my lord? The vampire uses his teeth to puncture the arteries in his victim's throat, and the marks upon your so lovely sister's throat give every appearance of just such an attack.'

'What shall we do, then?' I enquired.

'For now,' Sir Ulrich replied, 'we can do only what we are already doing. Your sister must continue to be careful of her sleep, for this is when the vampire is most wont to attack. The garlic is a strong deterrent against his attack. So is the little cross I gave her to wear. The vampire is unholy, so he fears that which is holy. And, from now on, perhaps it would be best, until we are able to hunt down this un-dead monster, if we keep watch over her room at night.'

I nodded. This was something I could do. Between the house staff, the stables, and the garden, there were more than a dozen men who could be enlisted to keep watch. They did not need to know they were looking for a vampire. It would be sufficient if they knew there was a threat to their mistress, and that they should be wary of anyone trying to slip into the house by night.

Later— The two doctors were persuaded to stay for supper. They made a somewhat incongruous sight at the dinner table. Not having planned to be there, they had not brought anything to wear, so there they sat, Doctor Allen in his black lounge suit, and Sir Ulrich in his old-fashioned black frock coat. My sister, and Miss Willis, wore appropriate gowns, and I had dressed in the proper formal attire.

The physicians were there to observe as much as they remained for any social reasons. Sir Ulrich, in particular, was keeping a careful eye on my sister. I was not sure what he was looking for, perhaps some peculiar mannerism, some clue that she was truly suffering from this metaphysical malady.

Shortly after dark, when the doctors were beginning to suggest that it might be time for them to leave, Lord Ravensbrook arrived. He seemed delighted to find the physicians here, and it soon became obvious why. On most evenings, when he visits, we sit in the parlour and chat. Now there were four men. Four, he noted, were enough for bridge.

Sir Ulrich and Doctor Allen, it transpired, played. We went into the card room and took our places at the table, the two doctors pairing up, which left me in partnership with the marquess.

I had noticed a sudden interest from Sir Ulrich when he learned of Lord Ravensbrook's strange skin condition. He seemed fascinated by a man who must, for his own safety, avoid the sunlight. Yet I noticed as well, his interest faded as suddenly as it had begun when, as we were walking down the hall to the card room, we passed an antique mirror. Sir Ulrich looked at the glass with considerable interest, but abruptly lost interest, both in the mirror and in Lord Ravensbrook, once that nobleman had passed behind him.

Ere he departed with Doctor Allen, he told me that he had, at first, suspected that our noble neighbour might be the vampire. My sister's malady seemed to correspond with his arrival at Winstead, and his 'allergy' to sunlight might mask the vampire's vulnerability to sunlight. But the mirror in the hall had put paid to those suspicions. He had seen the marquess, quite plainly, reflected in the glass.

XXII: Suzanne Willis's Diary

Wednesday, 24th July— I have just posted a long letter to my mother, letting her know that I will not be catching the late train to-night, but will stay on here at Muntglare until my dear friend has recovered her health. I feel that I cannot abandon her, though my darling Anna has informed me that I must move to another room. I will be just across the corridor from her, yet this seems so terribly far away.

This came about after a particularly bad night last night. Anna felt that she could not bear to wear the garlic garland, and instead slept with it beside her on the pillow. At first, I thought nothing of this, for she was her usual dear, affectionate self. We are always quite naughty now, and do not bother with even the usual light cotton night dresses we were careful to wear when I first came to this place. We sleep quite naked, most often wrapped in each other's arms.

So it was last night. The night was warm, and so were we. We decided to do something to cool off, so after O'Leary had helped her mistress to undress, Anna asked her to draw a tepid bath, which we would share.

The water was just right. Not so cool as to be uncomfortable, but not hot, either. We slipped into the big, vitreous china bathtub at opposite ends, for several minutes just resting in the water, leaning back against the smooth, cool surface and looking at each other. Though she has become frailer because of her strange malady, still my darling Anna is possessed of a lovely, enticingly perfect body. Her high, firm breasts, with their pink, slightly-puffy nipples, continue to entrance me. I love to suckle at those hard nubs, to tease them with my tongue, graze them playfully with my teeth.

At length, I moved towards her, rising up on my knees, lowering myself over her as she slipped down deeper into the warm water. Our breasts played against each other as our lips came together in a tender kiss. A tender kiss that quickly gained urgency, tongues coming into play. Hands roved over smooth, wet bodies. Our furry mounds pressed together, working sensuously, provoking those forbidden sensations. Fingers moved down, probed deeply, delving into the moist, slick depths, feeling occult muscles squeezing down, throbbing in a frantic rhythm as we made love in the water, the bathroom's tiled walls echoing with our cries of pleasure until we had once again worn each other out from climax after climax.

When we returned to our room, there was no energy remaining for love-making. Anna soon fell asleep, cradled in my arms, her dear head resting upon my shoulder.

I awoke, in the darkened room, to realise that Anna was once more engaged in that strange, erotic dream state, her arms and legs raised and circled, as if she were embracing a lover, her hips thrusting, her head thrown back in ecstasy, soft sobbing sounds emanating from her open mouth. I wanted to take hold of her, to shake her into wakefulness, yet found that I could not move.

With a final cry she again slumped, exhausted. The bed shook, as if someone were getting out of it, but there was no one there.

Anna rolled over, her arm draping across me. I could move now, and I took her into my arms and held her close to me. She seemed to be asleep, her breathing soft and regular.

We awoke shortly after dawn. My darling Anna was again lethargic, looking pale and unhealthy. Still, her hands on my body, and her lips on mine, told of renewed passion. She embraced me with a strange fervour, kissing me hard, grinding her body against me. Her lips trailed down my cheek, fastened upon my throat.

Suddenly she pushed herself away, crying, 'No!' quite loudly.

'What is it, dear Anna?' I asked, rather unnerved by her sudden change of attitude.

'No, I mustn't give in,' she said.

'Give in to what?'

She shook her pretty head, looking genuinely frightened of something.

'I think it might be best if you sleep in another room,' she said, very quietly. 'I fear for your safety if you stay here with me.'

'How?' I asked. 'Why?'

'Just now, I wanted to kiss your sweet lips. To kiss you all over, your lips, your throat, to let my lips explore your dear body, taste the sweet nectar of your arousal, to drink from the fount of your womanhood.'

'As I do you, my darling. What of it? Have you been suddenly stricken with some foolish moral compulsion?'

She shook her head. 'No. When I am with you, I care nothing for the conventions of morality, for the foolish rules that say I cannot make love to whomever I desire. No, sweet Suzanne, what made me recoil was a strange compulsion that I should bite rather than kiss. I wanted to sink my teeth into the soft flesh of your throat and drink the hot blood from the wound.'

As I write this, I ask myself, will I believe this a few years hence? What could have made my dearest friend even think of such a thing? It is so unlike her, for she is the dearest, gentlest creature ever God created to be a blessing to all she meets.

Later— I write this from my new room. From Anna's room, I could look out the window and across the great expanse of close-cropped grass leading down to the road. From here, the view is of the back garden, with its consciously rustic plan, the stables, and, beyond, the Old House, that great, gloomy mass of masonry and half-timbered stucco, which in the fading light appears as grim and fatal as that ancient Gothic pile which Poe sent tumbling into the dismal tarn with all the fatal Usher clan dying within.

To the good, Anna was not so seriously weakened as she was the last time she suffered one of those nocturnal erotic attacks. Indeed, she seemed much her old self during the day. Yet this, also, gives me reason to worry. The poor Cooper girl was said to be much improved only the day before she died. How can I not fear that my darling Anna may suffer the same grim fate?

I cannot help wondering if it was her sudden decision to forego the garland of garlic that brought this on. Doctor Heilger seemed very insistent upon that issue. I cannot imagine any reason why this should be the case, but I can think of nothing else. She has not suffered any of these strange psychic attacks when she wore the garland, but upon the first night she does not she is again attacked. If it was this, am I not culpable in failing to insist she don it, and not merely leave it on the pillow beside her?

Someone is rapping at my door. More later, perhaps.

XXIII: Maureen O'Leary's Diary

Thursday, 25th July— What an odd day this has been. I suppose I could say that this day's odd qualities began last evening. When I entered Lady Anna's room to prepare her for bed, she was somehow changed. She seemed colder, and rather sad. She has exiled Miss Willis to a room on the opposite side of the hallway, which I suppose must account for at least some of her melancholy. I can see how they complement each other, make each other complete. I doubt not that they must remain fast friends until they die.

'Oh, dear Maureen,' she said, as I unlaced her stays, 'I am desperately sad, yet I dare not risk my friend by allowing her to sleep with me ever again.'

I could tell by this that Lady Anna was deeply affected. She calls me by my Christian name at only two times, when we are intimate, or when she needs solace. I did not feel she wanted my caresses just then, so I knew it must be the other.

'Miss Willis would willingly risk all for you,' I replied. 'I am sure you know that. She is very fond of you, as am I.'

'I know. And I know that you would do the same, but I dare not risk her safety, nor will I risk yours. I do not know what is overtaking me, what terrible illness now tries to overmaster my resolve, my very being, but that it is powerful and evil.'

'You must not think such things, my lady,' I chided.

'I do not wish to. It is simply that I cannot avoid it. I see such terrible things in my mind's eye, and such strange, terrifying dreams come to me as I sleep.'

I finished loosening her laces and came around to stand in front of her, to unhook her stays. This was quickly accomplished, and I placed them aside for the night. I continued to undress her, pulling off her chemise, panta-lets, and hose, then fetching her night dress and helping her into it.

I found the garlic wreath on the chair next to her bed, took it up, and placed it around her neck. She seemed to shrink from the touch of the garland.

'Oh, must I wear this horrible thing?' she asked.

'Did you wear it last night?' I enquired.

She shook her pretty head, her shoulders slumping as she did so. 'No,' she admitted, 'I did not.'

'And this morning you were much the worse, were you not? Doctor Heilger insists that it is important you wear this when you sleep, and on the one night when you ignore his instruction, you relapse. Oh, my lady, you really must wear it.'

'But I can hardly bear the smell. It was merely oppres-sive last night, but this night it feels actually repulsive. Day by day, the odour grows more foul.'

'Nevertheless, my lady, you must wear it. His lordship insists that you must follow your physician's instructions, and that I must ensure that you do.'

At last, I convinced her. She reluctantly climbed into the bed and composed herself for sleep, with the garlic garland still resting around her neck. Satisfied that she would do as Doctor Heilger had instructed, I dimmed the lamps and left the room.

Noting that there was still light coming from beneath the door of Miss Willis's room, I softly knocked. After a moment, I heard footsteps, and she opened the door, a hastily-donned silk wrapper covering her night dress.

'Is Lady Anna well?' she asked, seeing me.

I nodded. 'So far as I can tell, yes,' I said. 'But I *am* concerned about her.'

Miss Willis opened the door wider. 'Please,' she said, 'do come in. She has banished me from her bed, you know, and I am concerned as well.'

'You are closer to her than I,' I said. 'It is only right that you would be concerned.'

'She makes love to you, as well,' Miss Willis declared. 'I have no monopoly where her favours are concerned.'

'Oh, my dear Miss Willis,' I said. 'It is not the same thing at all. When she makes love to me, I am quite aware that only desire is present, the compulsion to satisfy a physical need. And, as I have the same needs, well, I am content. But with you, there is so much more. With you, there is a passion that transcends the physical. The two of you have a spiritual connexion that is lacking 'twixt her and me.'

She sat down on the side of the bed. 'Please,' she said, 'when we are alone like this, do call me Suzanne. You are not my servant, though in our common concern for your mistress's fate, I do hope I may call you my friend.'

'Then you must call me Maureen,' I replied.

'I shall. Come, sit beside me.'

I sat on the side of the bed next to her. The windows were open, and a sliver of moon hung over the brooding bulk of the Old House.

'What shall we do about dear Anna?' Suzanne asked, looking terribly distressed. Who could blame her? She had been rejected by her dearest friend, and even though

Lady Anna might have the noblest of reasons for sending her from her bed, still, it must be frightfully painful. Whilst the mind argues reason and logic, and tells the heart that this is but a temporary separation, the heart may not wish to listen.

'She fears she might harm you,' I replied. 'If she sends you away, her motives are pure. She only wishes to keep you from danger.'

'Ah, my dear Maureen, I do not *care* if there is danger. She is my dearest friend, and has been so since the days we were at school together.'

Just then, I saw the oddest thing. Glancing out the open windows towards the Old House, I became aware of a great bat flapping purposefully towards us. His eyes must have caught the light through the window, for they seemed to glow with a preternatural redness. I must have gasped at this astonishing sight, for a moment later Suzanne had put an arm about my shoulders, and was watching along with me.

The bat continued to fly towards us for a few moments more, then, flapping furiously, rose upwards on its leathery wings, presumably to surmount the roof and fly over the house. I felt a strange chill as it did, for it seemed to me that those blazing eyes were looking directly into my soul, as if to steal some vital part of me.

'How very odd,' Suzanne said. Her remark was casual, but the way she said it told me that she had been just as unnerved as me.

'Did you note its eyes?' I asked.

'Like fire,' Suzanne replied. 'And such a large bat. Have you ever seen a bat so huge?'

'I wonder if it has escaped from a menagerie,' I said. 'None of our English bats are so large. None that I am aware of, at least. This seemed more like what our antipodean colonists sometimes speak of, their so-called "flying foxes," or some such giant creature.'

'I believe,' Suzanne said, rising and walking to the window, 'that, warm as it may be, to-night I shall sleep with the sash down.' She gave action to her word and closed the window. 'I do not relish the thought of that great creature flapping its way into the room.'

I rose, walked over to the window, and stood beside her, placing one hand on either of her shoulders in a comforting way. 'I quite agree,' I said.

Suzanne turned towards me, her deep green eyes peering into mine as she rested her hands on my hips. 'Stay with me to-night,' she said. 'I don't want to be alone.'

I nodded acquiescence. I had no particular desire to sleep alone, and staying with Suzanne would mean I was closer to my mistress's room.

Suzanne walked across the room and turned the gas jets low, but did not turn them off. When she returned, she helped me remove my clothing. As I would have to re-don my garments in the morning, I laid them carefully on a chair. Soon I was standing there beside the bed, quite as naked as I had ever been, for obviously I did not carry a night dress about with me when engaged in my regular duties.

'It seems unfair that you should be *au naturel*, and I clothed,' Suzanne commented. 'In some things, there should be no class distinctions.'

So saying, she slipped out of her wrapper, pulled her white cotton night dress off over her head, and stood before me, taking my hands in hers. 'There,' she said, 'now we are quite equal.' She looked down at my breasts. 'Well, perhaps not equal in all ways, but equal in raiment.'

We both looked out the window, perhaps suddenly conscious of our mutual nudity, and recalling what had transpired the last time we had been similarly disrobed. We walked closer to the window, looking out.

A movement in the garden caught Suzanne's eye. 'Is that someone standing there?' she gasped.

I peered out into the darkness. 'It may be,' I said.

We stood there for a moment, looking out into the garden, curious as to who, or what, might be out there. Then, as if in a mutual epiphany, we both seemed to realise that we were standing in front of the window quite as naked as the day we were born, with perhaps someone peering up at us from the darkness below.

Instinctively, each of us took hold of the drapery on our side of the window and drew it closed.

'I am sure that was a man standing in the garden,' I said.

Suzanne nodded. 'I wonder who it was. Was it Edwin, do you think?'

I shook my head. 'I doubt it. Lord Muntglare is, I shouldn't doubt, asleep in his bed by now. More likely, it was one of the servants. A groom, or a gardener, perhaps.'

'What do you suppose he saw?'

'Everything, I should think.' The window stool was only slightly above the level of my knees. Almost our entire bodies would have been visible from outside. Still, there was reason to hope at least some modesty had been preserved. 'Of course,' I added, 'the light is behind us, and there is only the faintest moonlight outside. I suppose, whatever he saw, it would have been a silhouette.'

Suzanne sat on the edge of the bed, looking relieved. 'I suppose you are right.'

She put her arm around my shoulders, letting her other hand rest on my thigh. Instinctively, I turned towards her. The subdued gaslight imparted a warm glow to her pale skin, and made her long, coppery-red hair seem like liquid fire as it fell about her smooth shoulders, and over her beautiful breasts. It struck me as slightly ironic, for here was Suzanne, beautiful, and as English as she could possibly be, with her exquisite green eyes and red hair, and me, child of Balbriggan, and brown hair and eyes so dark as to be nearly black.

She leaned towards me, her soft lips brushing mine. I placed one hand behind her back, pulling her closer, whilst the other cupped her breast. The hand on my thigh moved up, and I moved my legs apart, delighting as Suzanne's soft fingers brushed against my secret place. We fell back onto the bed, our lips still joined. Suzanne's legs were straddling my right thigh. I raised that knee, letting her grind her dear cunt against my thigh as her fingers continued to caress my tingling bud as it peeked from beneath its sensitive hood.

There was a sweet melancholy in our love-making. We both would have preferred to be making love to some-one else; the same someone else. We were together in our loneliness, in our sudden exile from the source of our happiness. Suzanne's desire was surely for dear Lady Anna, and, whilst my desire for my mistress was perhaps more purely carnal than Suzanne's, whose tender love for her dearest friend was obvious, still I missed her. Now, deprived of the fount of pleasure, we had come together for solace. The thrill of climax was bitter-sweet, satisfying the animal instincts that sought sexual pleasure in times of sorrow, but touching not the higher realm of the soul.

Still, it was physically satisfying, and it was pleasant to fall asleep in each other's arms. I knew that, in these cir-cumstances, Suzanne likely felt little in the way of passion for me. I was someone to cleave to in her sorrow at being parted from her lover, and this was acceptable to me, for if I was comforting her, she was comforting me.

I awoke while it was still dark, dressed, and quietly returned to my own room. I should have liked to have remained with dear Suzanne through the night, but my mistress's call bell was in my room, not her friend's. When she called for me in the morning, it was important that I be there to hear the bell and answer the call.

XXIV: Clipping from the High Coulston Record

ANOTHER UNUSUAL DEATH

BLOODLESS CORPSE FOUND

NEAR CHURCHYARD

25th July — Constable Simon, commencing his service on the Leicestershire Constabulary only two days ago, was presented with a shocking problem early this morning when he discovered the body of a young woman lying just outside the churchyard fence in front of Saint Wilfred's Church. The young constable immediately summoned his superior, Sergeant Churchill, who, in turn, summoned Inspector Royce. This reporter has learnt that the police initially suspected murder, but are now of the opinion that the killer may not be human.

'There was no blood,' according to someone close to the case. 'The poor girl's throat was half torn open, but there was no blood. Not on or around the body, and, strangest of all, apparently none in the body.'

'I think it must have been some sort of animal,' Inspector Royce suggested, 'though I cannot imagine what sort of creature would do so much damage and yet leave a bloodless corpse.'

"The High Coulston Horror," the village gossips

are calling the monstrous animal, whatever it may be. Those in the know are said to believe some large, vicious dog may be to blame. Others have suggested a lion, a leopard, or some other great cat, perhaps an unreported escapee from a menagerie.

The Coroner has scheduled an inquest, to be conducted in High Coulston upon Monday next. It is hoped that, by that time, the post mortem will have been conducted, and the police will have discovered who, or what, has committed this outrageous crime or, at the very last, have discovered who this mysterious young woman might be.

She is described as being about twenty years of age, five feet seven inches in height, weighing nine stone, with brown eyes and wavy brown hair that, let down, would fall to about the middle of her back. If anyone knows who this might be, it is requested that this information be passed on to the police.

XXV: Maureen O'Leary's Diary–Cont'd.

Thursday, 25th July, Later— My mistress was somewhat the worse when I answered her call and came up to her room to help her dress. She informed me that she had hardly slept at all. 'It was the garlic,' she said. 'It oppresses me, becomes more repulsive with every passing hour.'

'Nonetheless, mum, you must continue to wear the garland when you sleep. Sir Ulrich insists.'

'Still,' Lady Anna said, 'I suppose I must have slept, for I had the strangest dream. A great bat was flapping its leathern wings outside my window. And then, somehow, it was inside the room, where it flew around the room in a strangely purposeful manner before hanging inverted from the gasolier above my bed. It seemed to look at me reproachfully, and I instinctively knew that it was annoyed at the garlic garland about my neck.

'Something within me wanted to take the repulsive creature to my breast, as if it were a dear little kitten, and not some hideous denizen of the night. I could feel myself growing weaker, as if the mere presence of the creature was draining me of energy.

'After that, I remember nothing.'

I wondered what to make of this. Did this have something to do with the great, red-eyed bat that Suzanne and I had seen flying over the house? Should I mention that to my mistress? I was unsure on that point, but an answer soon presented itself when there was a soft rapping at the door and Suzanne entered.

'Tell her of your dream, Lady Anna,' I urged.

She did so, and Suzanne at once volunteered that she had seen just such an animal last night. She did not mention that I had been with her, which I thought might be for the best. I doubted my mistress would have been too upset by my mere presence in her friend's room—surely Suzanne would say nothing of the instinctive, meaningless love-making, lest it upset her lover—but it was not germane. Whether she saw the great bat alone, or in company, what mattered was that she had seen the bat.

'Could it have been real?' she asked.

We really had no idea of what the appropriate answer might be. That the bat could have spent a few moments outside her window was certainly possible. That it had entered through a closed sash and hung from the gasolier, well, that was another matter. Bats can wriggle through some very small openings, but a sealed sash must surely defeat them. It's not as if they can become incorporeal, after all.

XXVI: Doctor Allen's Journal

Thursday, 25th July — A most disturbing case in my surgery to-day. About half seven this morning, the police brought in the body of an attractive young woman of about twenty years. She appeared to have been killed by some animal, for her throat was torn open in a most savage manner, and all of the blood appeared to have been drained from her body.

Naturally, as he is still here, I decided to consult Sir Ulrich when I performed the post mortem examination requested by the police and by the coroner.

'I fear this confirms my suspicions,' Sir Ulrich informed me, when we were finished. 'There is a vampire at large in this village.'

I pointed the poor girl's throat. 'Surely this was an animal of some sort,' I protested.

'Then where is the blood? The police said there was no blood where she was found, and there was but little in her body. Where did it go?'

I pulled the sheet over the body and walked over to the sink to wash my hands. 'Did you not say that the sign of a vampire is the two small marks on the throat, made by the eye teeth? This poor girl's throat was torn out. There was no finesse.'

Heilger nodded sagely. He had been consulting his little book during the post mortem, occasionally nodding, or commenting that something was 'interesting.' Now he said:

'I believe this is a *new* vampire. One young in his ways, and perhaps desperate for his sanguine repast. One who has not learnt to hunt secretly yet.' He raised an eyebrow at a sudden thought. 'Or, perhaps, I should say "her" ways. Six days have passed since the poor Cooper girl was buried, and seven since your post mortem. Enough time, perhaps, for her body to have repaired the damage inflicted, if she prove to be one of those unfortunate victims of the un-dead who find themselves condemned to the same fate. If it be her, this would be her first vampire meal, and she would desperately need blood.'

'Even if this is so, what can we do?' I asked. 'We can hardly go to the police, tell them there is a vampire at large in High Coulston, and ask if they would be so kind as to dig up the recently-interred corpse of a shop girl because we think she has become a blood-sucking monster. They would laugh us from the premises, presuming they didn't summarily despatch us to Bedlam.'

'No, we must undertake this task ourselves. And, perhaps, we should also involve the Earl of Muntglare for this, more than anything else we could ever say to him, is evidence that what I fear has afflicted his sister is true. She is not the only victim.'

I could find nothing to contradict this suggestion. Lord Muntglare would certainly prefer to have proof, and not simply the speculation of one elderly physician. And it would give him hope. Sir Ulrich had told me that, according to what was written in Professor von Elbing's little book, if one could destroy the vampire who was preying upon the victim, the victim would almost instantly be restored to health and the curse would be lifted. Only if the victim had already become one of the un-dead would he remain so if his master were destroyed.

If we should discover that the poor Cooper girl was now one of this un-dead horde, it followed that the master vampire must be near. If the master vampire was near, then he could found and destroyed.

'I shall set the horse to the gig,' I declared. 'We shall drive out to Muntglare at once.'

XXVII: Lord Muntglare's Journal

Thursday, 25th July — I spent the morning with Anna. She is quite depressed to-day. Much of this is, I think, because she has banished her friend, Suzanne, from her bed. I have not formed a hard opinion of their relationship, un-natural though most would call it. Anna is so frightfully happy when they are together that I find it difficult to think ill of them. And now, when she has exiled Suzanne to another room, it is evident that she is the worse for the enforced separation.

'I hate that she must sleep in another room,' Anna told me. 'But I dare not allow her to remain here. I honestly fear that I might harm her.'

'I think she would take that risk,' I said. I had spoken to Suzanne earlier, and she had expressed exactly those sentiments.

'Perhaps she would, but I cannot allow her to do so. Oh, Neddy, there is some danger even during the day, so how much more must there be in the night. I am not in control of myself when I sleep. So long as I wake, I want to be near her, to breathe the same air, to partake of the same experiences, the same pleasures. Yet when I sleep, or, even worse, when I am in that twilight state where sleep and wakefulness merge, I experience the most over-powering urge not to kiss her, but to sink my teeth into the soft, white skin of her throat, and to drink in the hot red blood wherein dwells the essence of life.'

I must say, this statement took me aback. This was quite what Sir Ulrich had said of the vampire, that it lusted after blood, lived on blood. How could my sweet, gentle sister entertain such *outré* thoughts? Was she transforming into one of those blood-sucking monsters as I watched? She seemed strong enough, healthy enough, even though somewhat weakened. Was the weird contagion growing within her? And what, I wondered, could I do about it? Sir Ulrich's only cure was that we must destroy her vampire master, but we had not the least idea who that might be.

True, this all began when the Marquess Ravensbrook came to live in our midst, yet Sir Ulrich had ruled him out, for he clearly reflected in a looking glass, and I had, myself, seen him enjoy a good brandy or whisky. Admittedly, I had never seen him eat, but, where that was concerned, I had also never been in his presence at mealtime.

I left Anna with Suzanne. She is evidently comfortable enough with her friend during waking hours, for though she feels there is at least some danger then, it is during the night, when she is asleep, that she fears most for the safety of those dear to her.

The men I had posted about the grounds last night had nothing unusual to report. One of them, the groom, Curtis, at first gave an equivocal report, but when pressed admitted that he had seen something *in* the house, but not around it, before the draperies were drawn. From where he had been stationed, I had no doubt he had found a way to peep into Miss Willis's new room, and so reminded him of the tale of Tom of Coventry, struck blind for peeping at Godiva's naked ride through the city.

The man watching my sister's windows had seen nothing at all, though he did speak of a strange mist that seemed to descend over that wall early in the morning hours. I made nothing of this to the man, but decided that this was something that might interest Sir Ulrich.

I saw the man himself just before afternoon tea. He arrived in company with Doctor Allen, in the doctor's gig. As the afternoon newspaper had been issued just before they departed from the doctor's surgery, they brought that with them, for it contained an article touching upon their quest.

'Sir Ulrich is certain this is a vampire,' Doctor Allen declared, when we were alone in my library, and I had read the short article.

'The same creature you believe is tormenting my sister?'

'No, your lordship,' Sir Ulrich said. 'I believe this is a young vampire, one newly-fledged, to make use of the idiom, but almost certainly the thrall of the master vampire that we already seek. I suspect this is the late, lamented Miss Cooper, she that was buried upon the Saturday last.'

'Have you any proof?' I enquired.

'As yet, we do not. But I believe we can find all the proof we require if we conceal ourselves in the churchyard this evening. Then we can observe her as she rises from her grave.'

This was a novel idea to me. Even after Sir Ulrich had enlisted me in his vampire hunt, out of sympathy for my dear sister, I had not truly given much thought to how this was to be accomplished. How did one hunt for a vampire? I have no doubt that, had I given it more thought, I should have recognised that the most obvious way would be to determine where the vampire slept in his coffin during the day and break in there to kill him.

'I was at her burial,' I said. 'She is buried in the ground. How can she leave her grave? Were she interred in a crypt, certainly, I could conceive this. But does she dig her way out of the grave every night? Would this not result in an obvious disturbance of the earth above it?'

'Come with us into the village, your lordship,' Sir Ulrich suggested. 'There we may examine the grave as it is, take advantage of the redoubtable Mrs Dumphy's culinary skills, and, as it draws towards dark, take our posts in the cemetery.'

I nodded acquiescence, and went with them to the stables, after first informing my sister that I had to go into the village, and should not return home until quite late. The doctor's gig would seat but two people, so I had Jackson hitch Thunderer to the phaeton. I would drive it myself, I informed him. Sir Ulrich elected to ride with me, that we might talk at length during the drive.

When we reached the village, Sir Ulrich suggested that Doctor Allen go along to his surgery and inform his housekeeper that there would be an extra guest at supper, whilst he and I visited the cemetery. Doctor Allen agreed, taking his temporary leave of us.

We had to wait at the church, for it appeared that the late Miss Cooper's parents were visiting the grave, bringing freshly-cut flowers with which to adorn the temporary marker.

Josiah Cooper greeted me as they were leaving the churchyard. 'I just wanted to thank you, your lordship,' he said, 'and your lovely sister, for your attendance when we buried our poor Naomi. Your father was a very good man, arranging for me to finally purchase our farm, and at quite the reasonable price, and I can see those good qualities have come down to the next generation.'

'I felt it my duty to attend,' I replied, 'though you are no longer my tenants. I encountered your daughter many time in Mr. Elliott's book shop, and always found her to be a most delightful young woman.'

'She spoke well of you as well, your lordship,' Eloise Cooper declared. 'And of your sister. I hope she is well?'

'Well enough,' I replied. I saw no reason to disclose the truth, that my dear sister seemed to be following their daughter's course to decline and death.

They were soon on their way, plodding down the road in a donkey-cart. When they had driven out of sight, I went with Sir Ulrich to the grave.

The soil was still fresh, raised up in a low heap over the grave. It would no doubt be some months, or even years, before the mound subsided, to become once again level with the grassy surface.

Sir Ulrich knelt beside the grave, closely examining the fresh earth. At length, he motioned for me to come closer.

'Here, you see,' he exclaimed. 'Here, close together, these three round holes in the earth.'

'Are they not where the legs of a floral tribute once stood?' I asked. That was what they looked like to me. I pressed the tip of my stick into the soil, and it left a similar impression.

'Not at all, your lordship. If we could trace them, we would find these holes go down through the earth right to the coffin. These are how the vampire is able to leave her grave to go a-hunting, and to return after she has slaked her un-natural thirst.'

'But, how can a fully-grown woman travel through holes no more than half an inch in diameter? It isn't possible.'

'Your vampire is a very subtle creature,' Sir Ulrich explained. 'He can change his form to that of an animal, but he can equally become insubstantial, rising as a dank mist through these little holes, even using that form to pour himself under a door, or through the cracks around a closed window. This is why I asked your dear sister to wear the garland of garlic, for it should protect her even if the vampire gain entrance.'

I felt suddenly apprehensive. The watcher's mention of a strange mist near Anna's window in the night made me fear.

'Come,' Sir Ulrich said. 'We must make our way to Doctor Allen's home, for the faithful Mrs Dumphy will no doubt have begun her preparations for our evening repast.' He looked around. 'I only wish there were more trees and hedges in this churchyard. I fear it will be difficult to conceal ourselves when we return.'

'I know just the place,' I said. 'Over there, beneath those two oak trees. That is the Corwin family mausoleum. Five generations of my family are laid to rest in that little building, and I have the key. We can hide in there, with the door open, but still safely behind the iron gate.'

Friday, 26th July— The three of us returned to the churchyard just before dark. With my key, I unlocked the mausoleum and pushed back the heavy wooden door. Entering, I pulled the gate shut behind us. In the darkened churchyard, with the gate closed, no one would know that the door was open, and that we were waiting to spring out the moment the vampire appeared.

As we waited, I found my mind wandering back to happier days. Days when Mother and Father were still alive, and Anna and I had nothing to concern us beyond wondering whether to spend the day riding, or reading, or simply sitting in front of the hearth in the lounge doing nothing at all. If someone had told me then that I should one day find myself hiding in a mausoleum, waiting for a nightmare creature to appear, I would have thought them insane.

Yet, here I was. Behind me, in an ornate sarcophagus, lay the earthly remains of my fourth-great-grandfather, the thirteenth Earl of Muntglare, another Edwin, as it happened. It had been he who built this extravagant resting place, which now held five generations of my family, but would hold no more, for every niche but one was full, the floor by now consisted almost entirely of marble memorials, and the surrounding graves precluded further expansion of the structure to accommodate more burials. When my turn comes, or Anna's, we will be interred in a new mausoleum at Highgate Cemetery in London, large enough to suffice at least through the next century.

It was seven minutes before midnight, according to my watch, when I was startled to observe a body taking shape above Miss Cooper's grave. At first, there was only a tenuous ghost of a form, but it rapidly solidified. There could no longer be any doubt. This was Naomi Cooper, attired in the white gown in which she had been buried.

She stood there for a time, unmoving. Perhaps it was that this was still new to her, and the change from corporeal body in the grave, to incorporeal mist, and back again to tangible form had not become the ordinary thing that it no doubt was to the older vampire after hundreds or thousands of repetitions.

Yet, if she did not move, neither did we. Sir Ulrich, at the very least, had been convinced that this would happen, had been sure it was possible. Now, we were confronted with the reality. If Sir Ulrich had accepted this intellectually, it seems his reaction to the fact of it was no hastier than that of Doctor Allen and I, who were less sure of the possibility.

At length, we stirred, and Sir Ulrich pushed open the gate to the tomb. The vampire's head turned in our direction, but she made no effort to flee. Indeed, she merely watched as we approached, her expression curious, but shifting to recognition as we emerged from the shadows. In life, she had dealt with the doctor, and with me, many times in her capacity as clerk in Mr. Elliott's book shop.

I suppose we did not seem much of a threat to her. Sir Ulrich carried a sharp wooden stake and a heavy mallet. A vampire should have feared this, yet even this infant amongst the vampire sort could recognise how little threat was genuinely presented. Staking a vampire whilst he slept in his coffin was no doubt a simple enough task. Trying to drive a stake through a wide-awake, fully-mobile vampire would be much more difficult.

As for the doctor and myself, I knew he had a revolver in his pocket. All I had was my stick, which I was gripping in my left hand, just below the ferrule, as we approached.

'Lord Muntglare,' Miss Cooper—I feel I must still so style her, for, dead, alive, or un-dead, that is who she remains—said, by way of greeting. 'What brings you to this dismal place so early of a morning?' She looked around quickly. 'And with such distinguished companions! Doctor Allen, my good friend. And, another. I fear I do not know this gentleman, with his fierce expression and that dangerous-looking stick in his hand.'

'Miss Cooper,' I said. I found it impossible to break the conditioned habit of courtesy to a beautiful young woman. In life, Miss Cooper had been quite attractive. Petite, slender, with startling green eyes and auburn hair, and a dazzling smile that would turn the heart of any man. In death—in un-death, rather—she was even more lovely. I knew this was not truly the Naomi Cooper I had known these many years, but only a malevolent spirit, animating her cast off shell, and holding prisoner her immortal soul, yet something about her now seemed to radiate a kind of glamour. Not the ordinary sort, whereby the reader of popular periodicals describes a beautiful woman, but the Scottish sort, which has less to do with beauty than with an un-natural fascination.

'I must apologise for what happened to that poor girl,' she said, sounding quite sincere. 'I was newly-risen, and our friend, the doctor here, did considerable damage to my physical form during his post mortem.' She smiled benignly at the doctor. 'I do not hold you in any way guilty, for you were merely doing what was expected of you under the circumstances. Still, it required a huge amount of psychic energy to restore my body to its former state, indeed, to *regrow* those parts you did not replace in my body before stitching me back up.'

She looked at me again. 'I am sorry if what I say is, perhaps, a bit out of place in a woman, but the doctor must know that the damage he did was not permanent. And that I only killed that poor girl because of necessity. I needed a great deal of blood. Too much, it seems, at least for her. I assure you, gentlemen, I did not intend for her to die.'

'Who was this poor girl you murdered?' Sir Ulrich demanded.

Miss Cooper shook her head. 'I do not know. Within minutes of arising for the first time, I heard a train coming into the station. I rushed over there, and found the girl travelling alone in a private compartment. I simply asked her to follow me, and she did. I mastered that skill almost at once. She followed me back here, and just outside the fence I took her blood and, unfortunately, her life. I suppose you may find reassurance in that, because it was done so quickly, she will never become what I am. She is simply dead and will remain so.'

Doctor Allen looked at the girl, then at me, and finally at Sir Ulrich. 'What shall we do now?' he asked. I knew his problem. Though now of the un-dead, Miss Cooper was speaking to us in a reasonable manner, acknowledging her guilt, but putting forward necessity, coupled with inexperience, as justification. To the vampire, after all, a human victim is simply a meal, and I suppose they feel no more guilt at taking a blood meal from a living human than I would in eating a steak. The doctor, whose whole life was devoted to *saving* life, was now baulking at taking one. And, perhaps, her unearthly beauty also deterred him.

'We must destroy the monster,' Sir Ulrich said, brandishing the stake.

Miss Cooper's response was a gay laugh. 'Do you call me a monster, sir? True, I took a life. A single life. I do not expect to take any others. I am fully restored, you see, and need only a little blood, from time to time, to maintain myself in health.' She glanced at me, looking rather pitiable. 'It need not even be human.'

'Do not give in to her, my lord,' Sir Ulrich said. 'She will beguile you, so that you do not destroy her, and then she will come and kill you and yours. Worse, she will make you into another like her, the un-dead, spreading like a plague over the land.'

'Were that the case,' Miss Cooper objected, 'this land should long ago have been filled with vampires. Yet we are few, or so my master says, and his is the wisdom of the ages, for he has lived hundreds of years. Do not think us cursed, but consider that we have received the gift of eternal life.'

'Bah!' Sir Ulrich grunted. Without an outward sign of warning, he suddenly thrust with the sharpened stake.

If his intent was to thrust it through the vampire, he failed. The sharpened point grazed her arm, tearing the sleeve of her dress, but apparently leaving her unharmed.

'Enough,' she cried. 'If you will persist, then you leave me no choice.'

She lashed out at Heilger. He had warned of the vampire's un-natural strength, and now he became the victim of it. Her little fist took him on the corner of the jaw and he dropped like a poleaxed steer.

Doctor Allen produced a revolver from his pocket and raised it, but before he could fire she had wrenched it from his hand and thrown it far across the churchyard. She pushed him down, straddling his hips, and holding his shoulders down with her hands.

'Could *you* not have been kind?' she demanded. 'In life, I used to anticipate your visits to the shop, hoping, always, that I would be there to serve you. I even thought, of a time, that you determined your visits to the shop by my schedule, for Mr. Elliott told me that you never came by at any other time. I could so easily have loved you, even as I am.' She shook her head. 'But now, now there can be only war, and so you must suffer and become one of us.'

She threw back her head, opening her mouth wide. The sharp, over-grown canine teeth in her upper jaw gleamed in the subdued moonlight.

It seemed that she had momentarily forgot me. Without thinking, I twisted the top of my stick above the ferrule. There was a slight click as the catch released, and I whisked away the lower tube to reveal the slim, twenty-inch Sheffield-steel blade concealed within.

She heard the click, and rose up on her haunches, turning towards me, a look of pure animal hatred in her blazing green eyes. But it was too late for her. I swung the blade, and the razor-sharp weapon sliced cleanly through her neck.

Her head toppled off her body, bearing a look of utter astonishment. Great gouts of blood fountained from her neck, drenching the unfortunate doctor, as her lithe body slowly toppled over and lay lifeless on the ground.

Doctor Allen got up, and helped Sir Ulrich to his feet. 'Now what do we do?' he asked. 'She is dead, but we cannot put her back in her grave. Not without the risk of re-digging the grave, which would surely be noticed.'

'We will put her in the mausoleum,' I said. 'There is one empty niche, and with the new mausoleum completed at Highgate, it will never be filled. Let us place her in it, seal it up, and she may rest with my ancestors until the final trumpet.'

The others agreed that this would be the most logical solution, so Doctor Allen and I took up her headless body, and Sir Ulrich collected her head. We took her into the mausoleum, and I showed them the empty niche at the back.

We placed her body in the niche. Sir Ulrich put her head there, propping it up on the severed neck, so that the lifeless eyes looked down the length of her body. Together, the three of us then lifted the blank marble slab into place, sealing the niche, and so concealing the now true-dead corpse of Naomi Cooper.

With the niche sealed with its marble slab, we left the mausoleum, locked the door and gate, and slipped quietly from the churchyard to make our way back to Doctor Allen's surgery. Fortunately, we passed no one on the way, as we kept to the alleyways. The streets of High Coulston are only poorly-lit at night, but with the doctor's clothing drenched in the vampire's blood, obviously it was for the best if we did not have to explain this. It was well, I thought, that we were dressed almost entirely in black, which in the poor light might not show the blood stains.

'It was fortunate that you carried a sword-stick,' Sir Ulrich said, after we were safely back in the surgery. 'I fear we did not plan sufficiently.'

'This stick is a faithful companion,' I replied. 'I do not go out at night without it.'

Doctor Allen had gone to his room to wash himself, and to change his clothing. He returned now, wearing trousers, a shirt without the collar attached, and bedroom slippers on his stockinged feet. Even cleaned up, it was obvious he had suffered from his brush with death.

'Did we do the right thing?' he asked. 'Might we not have believed her, that the one death was inevitable, and that there would be no others?'

'This is the residue of her glamour,' Sir Ulrich replied. 'She would say such a thing to facilitate an escape, but she would not keep her word. She has bewitched you, to use the old term.'

'She was right, though. I *could* have loved her. When she was alive, there were times when I thought that I did, and hoped that she might one day care for me.'

'A vampire would not make a good wife,' Sir Ulrich offered. 'The vampire is a creature of the purest sensuality, which is what makes them so attractive, though what they are should naturally repel. Even though she might care for you, you would be tempting fate. Her nature must ultimately exert itself and you would be lost.'

I took out my watch. It was a quarter past three in the morning. Not only had our adventure taken nearly six hours, but it occurred to me that I had forgot to wind my watch, and it must surely run down if I did not do so. And it was that simple act of opening the back of the case, taking the key from the chain, and winding the mechanism that finally brought me out of the strange reverie that had occupied my mind all of that night, and most of this morning.

'It is time for me to return to Muntglare,' I said.

'Are you sure?' Doctor Allen asked. 'You could stay here for the rest of the night. You are tired, and it is a long drive.'

I smiled. 'Thunderer knows the way, should I drift off. If I give him his head, I will certainly awaken in my own stables, if I do not wake again during the journey.'

The first hint of dawn was tinging the eastern sky by the time I was home, had seen to Thunderer, and retired to my rooms. I gave my valet strict orders that I was not to be disturbed before noon, except in a dire emergency, and dropped into bed.

XXVIII: Lady Anna Corwin's Journal

Friday, 26th July — Neddy was gone most of the night. He returned early this morning, left instructions not to be disturbed, and retired to bed. Except in some great emergency, he was not to be awakened before noon. I shall have to ask him what sort of adventure he was absent on, and did it involve a girl?

My own night was a strange one. I retired shortly after ten o'clock last evening. Dear Suzanne once again implored me to let her sleep in my room, but again I insisted that she would be safer in her own until this strange malady may be cured.

As it was a hot night, and I am still forced by Sir Ulrich's orders to sleep with the windows tightly shut, I decided to sleep nude, with only the sheet over me. I have done this more often of late, and particularly when Suzanne was still able to share my bed. It is a wonderful feeling, to sleep naked, snuggled against the body of a beautiful friend.

I found myself thinking of Suzanne as I struggled to sleep. I was strangely anxious. My brother was away on some adventure. My friend was banished to another room. My lady's maid was, no doubt, asleep in the servants' quarters. I longed for someone to talk to, to tell my problems. Without thinking, I found my fingers working in my quim. The best cure for anxiety, I have always believed, is what the doctors call therapeutic massage to hysterical paroxysm. Surely that was what I needed if I were to get any sleep.

I was quite wet, and soon had two fingers inserted into my secret cave of desire, massaging the slick, sensitive flesh, whilst the heel of my hand pressed rhythmically against the hooded pink bud wherein feminine pleasure seems to reside. I raised my fingers to my lips, licking off the musky sweet juices, savouring the taste, the texture, before re-inserting my fingers.

My fingers moved faster now, my hand pressing harder, and I could feel the dark repository of unbridled lust begin to contract, squeezing my fingers, whilst every muscle in my body seemed to tense and thrill with ecstasy. I know I was moaning, panting softly, my hips rising from the bed, until that sudden release of tension when I collapsed onto the mattress in exhaustion.

After that, I was able to sleep. For how long, I know not. Sometime during the night I had again that strange, erotic dream. Once more my room filled with thick mist, and when it cleared, Lord Ravensbrook was once again standing over me, naked, his manhood thick and hard, his eyes compelling.

I pulled off the garlic, for I know, in my dreams, that he finds it unpleasant. He stood by the bed. I lay on my side, facing him, taking his generative organ between my lips. The thick shaft slid easily in and out of my hungry mouth. I wondered what it would be like if he shot his spunk into my mouth. He has never done so, but always mounts me before that can happen.

He did so again this morning, climbing onto the bed and lowering himself into me, thrusting deep, stretching me with his huge, steely rod as he lavished his hot kisses on my mouth, my breasts, and my throat.

As his lips touched my throat I tensed, waiting for the sweet pain that always came with this. But this night the dream ended differently. Just as he was about to fully consummate our somnolent union he suddenly raised himself above me on his arms. He said something I did not understand. A single word, perhaps a name, though certainly not mine. Then:

'They have killed her!'

With that, he vanished, dissolving into mist yet again, leaving me desperately unsatisfied. I could not tell if this was all part of a dream, or if it was real. Surely, I thought, this aching desire was not merely a nocturnal fantasy? The mist having dissipated, I felt sure that I had awakened, but could not recall consciously throwing off the sheet, nor drawing my legs up in so wanton a posture. I only knew, with what could only be conscious certainty, that my privates were quite wet, and my desire was sharper than ever. Again, I put my fingers to use, rubbing, probing, exploring intimately, until, at last, my body was again pulsing and shaking in the grip of pleasure. And yet, though it seemed that I had attained some sort of erotic peak, and my climax left me so thoroughly spent that I could not even lift an arm once I had let it drop to the mattress beside me, it was somehow less satisfying this time.

When I awoke shortly after eight o'clock this morning, I felt wonderful. That is, until I sat up, threw my legs over the side of the bed, and started to walk to the chair where I had thrown my night dress when I decided last night that I would sleep *au naturel.* Though I felt full of energy, my limbs moved only sluggishly. It was as if I had the energy of one my own age, but the body of an elderly crone. Was this some new manifestation of my strange illness? I wanted to move quickly, felt I should do so, yet could only force my body to reluctantly perform a desired action.

I rang for O'Leary, once I had managed to pull on my night dress. She soon arrived, and so began the tedious routine of dressing. I cannot avoid thinking that it must be so much simpler to be a man.

There was a moment of mutual embarrassment when O'Leary reached for a hair brush and clearly noticed the paper-covered novel lying next to it on my dressing table. I had been reading it in my loneliness, and I fear it is not the sort of thing a girl brought up in a sheltered Irish village would encounter, for it is quite exotic and sensual.

'It is a very naughty book,' I admitted. 'I read from it when I feel blue, you see.'

O'Leary nodded, smiling knowingly. Perhaps her literary tastes are broader than I had thought, though I have seen her room, and the little library she maintains there runs heavily to poetry and popular novels.

'I am sure it is a fine novel, your ladyship,' she said, brushing my hair.

Once I was dressed, and O'Leary had finished her inspection and tidying of my room and returned to the servants' quarters, I picked up the little book and placed it in a drawer. I still can't imagine why I left it out where someone could find it. I am sure Neddy reads far worse, but I have no idea of Suzanne's literary tastes, and it was certainly a *faux pas* of the worst sort to let a servant discover it. I do not fear for O'Leary's discretion, naturally, for if she has never disclosed the things we sometimes do, certainly she will not gossip about what I read.

I wonder, is this strange illness brought on by my behaviour? Women are expected to behave in certain ways in this fifty-eighth year of our good queen's reign, and those ways do not include erotic liaisons with best friends and lady's maids. It is, perhaps, somewhat less horrible than such behaviour in a man. Poor Oscar Wilde now languishes in Pentonville Prison for his relationships with young men, but I cannot recall ever hearing of a woman suffering a similar fate.

Still, the good Lord cannot approve of what I have done, even if there is nothing in His word that explicitly forbids it, as there is for the similar transgressions of men. When darling Suzanne worships my dear cunt with her tongue I am transported with sensual pleasures, and surely God hates such pleasures. It is not the place of a woman to derive any sort of pleasure from a sexual act, for her role is to be the receptacle, to marry, and tolerate a man's animal lusts and nothing more.

Will the day come when women may plainly express their own carnal desires? Or would even the suggestion be such a horrible breach of propriety that it may never be considered?

Suzanne has just come in. I shall resume later, if there is more to say.

XXIX: Suzanne Willis's Diary

Friday, 26th July— Poor Anna presents a strange disparity of symptoms today. Mentally, she seems much improved. Physically, she is certainly weaker. I am at a loss as to what to do. I should have gone home on Wednesday, yet here I remain, two days later, ever the faithful friend and companion, though for now banished from sleeping in the same bed with my dearest friend.

I do not consider what I did with dear Maureen on the Wednesday night to be an impediment to my loving relationship with her mistress. No, that was purely physical, a mutual hunger that required satisfaction. A greater impediment would be what happened under that great forest oak with Edwin. Still, I doubt not that, though he flirt with me, yea, even though we may be intimate, he will at length choose a more appropriate match. I have little to offer him beyond a physical craving, and what some would certainly consider an un-natural affection for his sister. Should I marry, I will bring no dowry, no wealth, and no property. If I marry, it must be for love, for that is all I have to offer, and, while I find in Edwin an admirable gentleman, and possessed of a handsome physical endowment, I do not love him.

Besides, should I ever even consider marriage, I would always wonder if it was out of some passionate attraction to the Earl, or because such a union would find me a permanent resident of Muntglare, and so closer to my beloved Anna. Anna, whose soft lips feel so perfect when pressed against my own. Anna, whose blond-bordered womanliness, parted at the liquid pressure of my curious tongue, wells forth the sweet nectar of her passion.

Anna, who is now in thrall to some strange malady that saps her strength, even as it inflames her sleeping passions, and wastes her strength in vigorous coupling with a phantom presence. In ancient times, the superstitious spokes of the succubus and the incubus. Now, I can almost swear that, at least of the latter, there is tangible evidence in my dearest friend, whose bouts with her invisible lover always leave her weaker.

Is this what the ancients meant? Was the incubus some phantom, immaterial, unseen, yet still tangible to the victim?

'I feel so weak,' Anna said. 'I cannot understand it. I feel both full of energy, yet hardly able to move.'

'Did you dream again last night?' I asked.

Anna nodded an acknowledgement. 'The same, yet different. It was the same in that it was our good neighbour, Lord Ravensbrook, materialising quite nude, and with his magnificent member thrust proudly before him. Yet it was also different, for though I took him in my mouth, and then within me, he did not complete the act, as, in my dreams, he has always done before. No, my dear, just as I was approaching the heights, he suddenly stopped, muttered something about someone having "killed her," and post haste faded away and was gone, leaving me quite unsatisfied.'

'Who is "her," do you know?' I asked.

'No.' She shook her head. 'I have no idea, nor of who were the killers. It is just another mystery to add to this strange malady.'

'You should tell your brother of this,' I suggested.

'No, dear, that I cannot do. It would embarrass me too greatly.'

'Tell Doctor Allen, at least. He is a physician, so whatever you say to him, he has keep in confidence.'

'Perhaps,' she said, in a tone of voice that did not inspire any confidence she would do so.

I looked out the window, over the broad expanse of green lawn, spotted here and there with artistically-sited trees and shrubs. The grounds were a tribute to the landscape architect Anna's father had employed to create a natural setting, some thirty years in the past, when the old formal gardens had become passé.

'What if we have a horse hitched to the dog cart and take it out for a jaunt?' I asked. 'I know that you are a skilled driver. Or I can handle the reins, if you don't feel up to it.'

Anna smiled for the first time that morning. 'Yes,' she said, 'I think that would be a brilliant idea. I can have cook pack a hamper, and we can drive out into the country and take our luncheon *al fresco*. Yes, an excellent idea. And I feel certain I am strong enough to drive, with you there to relieve me if need be.'

My darling Anna seemed to come back to life as we walked out to the dog cart, which the groom, Curtis, had hitched to a tractable three-year-old Friesian mare called Cleo. They are such magnificent beasts, with their black coats and flowing manes, and make wonderful carriage horses.

I noticed Curtis looking at me oddly, and I must say that it made me feel more than a little uncomfortable. He displayed a surprisingly superior expression, though he was properly subservient to Anna. I could think of no reason for his attitude, but decided to say nothing just then, not wishing to upset my friend, whose condition was already delicate enough.

The hamper, and an old blanket to serve as a ground cloth, went into the dog box. We climbed up onto the seat, and Curtis passed the reins to Anna, who took them expertly, snapped them sharply, and guided the ebon mare out of the stable yard and down the long drive to the road.

Getting out into the summer air, and driving the beautiful animal, did wonders for Anna's spirits. We drove well out into the countryside, passing Winstead, with its gloomy old house, still unchanged even now that Lord Ravensbrook was in residence. We continued on past the Cooper farm, where the unfortunate girl had lived whose symptoms seemed so much like my friend's. On and on we drove, finally taking the horse and dog cart off the road near a stone bridge and following the brook for perhaps half a mile until we came to a secluded spot where a grove of trees came down to the brook, and provided a bit of privacy for anyone stopping there.

Anna applied the hobbles to the horse, leaving her free to graze on the rich grass. Between the hobbles, and the dog cart she was still harnessed to, there was little chance she would try to wander away.

I spread the blanket on the ground near the brook, and Anna brought the hamper. Cook had packed it with wooden plates and cups, cheap tin utensils, and an estimable choice of delicacies for our meal. There was a roasted chicken, a loaf of freshly-baked bread, thinly-sliced beef, cheeses, ham, mustard, and two bottles of wine, a German white, and a French red. We would eat well, we decided. Naturally, we set to the food as quickly as we could, for it was a warm day, and we did not wish to take the risk that anything should start to turn bad before we had a chance to eat it. There was little risk to the cheese or wine, but we were naturally wary of the meat and chicken, so we constructed sandwiches and enjoyed a hearty lunch as only two women, freed from the sight of men, may do.

Finishing, we packed whatever remained back in the hamper, and put it back into the dog box. We left the blanket on the ground for the moment, lying back upon it, our upper bodies raised, resting on our elbows, looking down at the brook as it rippled its way towards the Avon.

'I feel so much better for this,' Anna declared. 'I think this was what I needed, to get out of the house and into the open air of the countryside. Someplace where there is no smell of garlic in the air, and no doctor telling me what I must do.'

'I am glad to hear that,' I said. 'Perhaps we should do this daily, until your malady is cured. Who can say? Perhaps all you needed was the fresh air and sunshine.'

'Fresh air, sunshine, and you,' she said, gazing into my eyes.

'Indeed.'

We leaned towards each other, our lips coming together in a tender kiss that soon grew in passion and intensity. Anna lay back on the blanket, our lips never parting as I turned above her. I could feel her tongue slipping into my mouth and responded in kind. Though we had been separated only a couple of days, and still in the same house, if not the same room, still it was like being reunited with a lover after months of separation.

My hand ran down her body and began to pull up her skirt and petticoats, and I could feel her doing the same to mine. These were the times when I cursed fashion's requirements for long skirts and multiple layers of petticoats and pantalets beneath them. Oh, for the freedom of Eve's day, before the Fall, when she and Adam could gambol in Eden without shame, naked and free.

Her fingers found my secret place and began to caress me. I returned the favour, and was delighted to find her growing quickly wet as my fingers traced the outline of her hidden lips, probed between them, delved deeply into her moist, quivering depths.

Oh, it was as if the forced estrangement of the last days had never been. No, more than that, it was as if we were again making love to each other for the first time, as on that first night when I had arrived in High Coulston on the train after three year's separation, not knowing if the intimacy we had shared at school would be renewed.

I fear we were quite loud, unconfined in the open air, far from prying eyes and ears. With no one to disturb, we cared not at all if the birds and the forest animals heard the cries of our renewed passion.

And yet, our love-making ended not with some grand climax, though certainly our bodies were wracked with passion, but with raucous laughter, for as the paroxysms of love began to wane we heard a snicker, and looked up to find dear Cleo, dragging the dog cart behind her, come to see what all the noise was about. The curious expression on the horse's long face was irresistible, and both of us lost what little composure we had left and dissolved into gales of laughter.

XXX: Maureen O'Leary's Diary

Saturday, 27th July— My mistress was much refreshed when I came to dress her this morning. Her jaunt yesterday with her friend has done her a world of good. She is much more like her usual self to-day.

There is some interesting gossip in the servants' quarters. One of the gardeners, who lives on a small holding of his own, and not on the estate, reports that there is a rumour in the village of another young girl suffering a similar affliction to Lady Anna and the poor Cooper girl. It would appear that, whatever this strange malady may be, there is more than one form. Like Miss Cooper, the village girl seems to be failing very quickly, whilst the form attacking Lady Anna seems not so virulent, acting as a chronic, rather than an acute affliction. It appears that not much hope is being held out for the girl.

I received another letter from my publisher to-day, enclosing another cheque, this time in the amount of £18/4. I shall take this to the bank come Monday. He is asking for another book, perhaps the further exploits of Cecily Freelove, the heroine of *The Erotic Adventures of a Lady's Maid.* Heaven knows, there would be great heaps of inspiration in this house since dear Suzanne's arrival, were I foolish enough to make use of it. No, I shall have to rely upon my imagination once again, lest Lady Anna, or some other reader, connect me with these novels. It is one thing to write about the forbidden, but quite another to have it generally known that you do.

I suppose I should be grateful to my mistress, though, for her contribution to my growing bank account. It is quite possible that, of that most recent cheque, tuppence came from her purchase. With this latest remittance, the total I have on deposit will amount to £321/7/9, which I have to say is far more than I ever expected to possess.

The bell is ringing. I must go.

Later— Lord Ravensbrook called shortly after sunset. Naturally, I was not generally present as he visited, but my mistress and Miss Willis described his visit at length as I was preparing Lady Anna for bed. It seems his lordship was upset about something, though he would not say just what it was.

'Often,' Suzanne said, 'I think that we British are too reticent when it comes to what is closest to us.'

'I quite agree,' Lady Anna responded. 'Lord Ravensbrook's bare statement that he had recently lost a friend through misadventure means nothing if he is not forthcoming with who the friend might have been, or what sort of misadventure.'

'I could not escape the feeling,' Suzanne continued, 'that this "misadventure" might have been a deliberate attack, and that his lordship might be planning some sort of revenge. I should not wish to be the object of such an attack. There is something dangerous about him, I think.'

I was wondering if I should speak. We had discovered something about Lord Ravensbrook's household in the servants' quarters, which suggested things were somewhat odd in that old house.

'He is quite handsome, of course,' Lady Anna said. 'And obviously very wealthy, which in these days of massive death duties is becoming unusual for old families.'

'I am not so sure of that, your ladyship,' I offered. 'He may have less than he seems.'

'What makes you say that?' Lady Anna asked.

'It is something I heard. It appears that, in that big house, he has but a single servant, an elderly butler who also serves as his coachman. This suggests the sort of frugality one might expect in a man living well beyond his actual means.'

'Is this true?' Suzanne asked.

'I have it from Mrs Irving, who has it from Jackson, who heard it from the farrier. His lordship does not seem to keep a proper staff, but brings in people as needed from the village to maintain the grounds, or care for his animals. No one, it seems, is ever permitted inside the house.'

'How very odd,' Lady Anna said.

'It is only what I have been told,' I said. 'But think; he visits here frequently, yet, has he ever invited you, or his lordship, to reciprocate? If there are no servants, he would naturally wish to avoid having visitors and so revealing this.'

'Of course,' Lady Anna said, 'you'll not gossip about this — to anyone else.'

'Naturally not, your ladyship.'

I learn many secrets in my position. I would not keep it for long were I to go about revealing them. Nor would my life be as interesting, or as easy. A lady's maid, after all, is far less burdened with duties than an ordinary maid. Though her hours may be longer, they are less filled with work, and offer ample time for reading, sewing, and other less tedious things. Truth be told, we are not always well-liked by the other maids, who may resent the amount of leisure time we appear to have.

A few minutes later, I had Lady Anna into her night dress, had put away those things that needed to be put away, and collected a few soiled items that would go into the washing. My work done for the night, I returned to the servants' quarters, leaving the two friends still conversing. The soiled clothing was deposited in the laundry, and I entered my room, closed the door, and turned the lock.

It took me only a few minutes to remove my own clothing. In addition to the letter from my publisher, I had received a package from an artist in Blackpool, which had come by courier, and not by way of the Royal Post. Now I opened this, and was pleased to find that the glassy ceramic *objet d'Arte* had come through in perfect condition.

It is a lovely, ten-inch long ceramic image of a man's rampant weapon, and quite detailed though, of course, the genuine article is not covered with a vitreous glaze. I had not bothered to pull on my night dress after disrobing. Now I lay myself down on my bed, drew up my legs, and began to tease my pearl of passion with the new toy.

My fingers dipped inside me, pulling musky juices from within and rubbing them where most needed. The glassy glaze coating the beautiful phallic figure became extremely slick, and with little effort the lovely thing penetrated deep within me, stretching the inner walls of my womanly recesses. I slid it in and out to what I realised, with a soft chuckle, to be a strict waltz rhythm, each stroke a little easier, a little smoother, as the ceramic godemiche became wetter and wetter with my hot juices.

My hooded pearl was throbbing with sensual pleasure, peeking out, welcoming my wetted fingers as they toyed with it. I was climaxing so strongly that I had to push extra-hard to keep the fat dildo from being expelled by the frantic contractions of my quim. Over and over again my body writhed in carnal passion until, at last, I fell into an exhausted sleep with my new toy still thrust up inside me.

XXXI: Report of the Coroner's Inquest

Monday, 29th July— The proceedings were called to order at 10 o'clock in the morning on this date, Alton Williard, Esq., Coroner for High Coulston, presiding, and Mssrs. Dorring, Alister, Edmunds, and Fuller empanelled as jury. Called to give evidence were Inspector Royce, Sergeant Churchill, and Constable Simon of the Leicestershire Constabulary, High Coulston District, and George Allen, MB BS, contract police surgeon for High Coulston.

Having been sworn, Constable Simon detailed the events surrounding the discovery of a dead body outside the fence surrounding Saint Wilfred's Church early in the morning of 25th July. Sergeant Churchill, and Inspector Royce were then called in turn, and each gave evidence. All three were of the opinion that the deceased had been the victim of some sort of animal attack, though none had any fixed opinion as to what sort of animal might have been involved.

Inspector Royce entered into evidence that the deceased was Miss Alice Milton, age 18 years, two months, and four days at the time of her death, and that she had been positively identified by her mother. Miss Milton was a resident of Leicester, and had been reported missing to the police in that town when she failed to arrive on her scheduled train from London. Neither her mother, nor the police, were able to provide any obvious reason why

Miss Milton should have left the train in High Coulston, particularly as she left her bags and reticule in her compartment. Inspector Royce was forthcoming in crediting Doctor Allen for the suggestion that, as the girl was unknown to anyone in this village, she might have arrived by train, and might be identified by enquiring as to any passengers who failed to arrive at their destination anywhere along the line.

Doctor Allen was himself then sworn. He related the results of the post mortem, which he conducted with Sir Ulrich Heilger, KCB, DPhil, MD, FRS. Doctor Allen deposed that, in his opinion, the police were correct in speculating that the deceased was killed by some unknown animal. Sir Ulrich has returned to London, but left a sworn statement concurring with Doctor Allen as to the cause of death.

The members of the jury concurring, a ruling of Death by Misadventure was entered, in that the deceased was mauled by an animal or animals, type unknown, and that unless the guilty beast may subsequently be identified as a domestic animal previously known to be dangerous, no criminal charges are warranted, and the body of the deceased shall be released forthwith to her nearest of kin.

XXXII: Suzanne Willis's Diary

Tuesday, 30th July— I was shocked when I entered my darling Anna's room this morning, shortly after the hall clock struck nine. I had come in answer to frantic knocking on my door, for it was Maureen who discovered my friend collapsed on her bed.

'I cannot wake her,' Maureen told me, the shock strong on her lovely Irish face.

I hurried across the hall, and there she was, stretched out on her back atop the sheets, her night dress crumpled on the floor beside the bed, naked, arms and legs spread in a most indecent manner. I could see her beautiful breasts slowly rising and falling, so I knew she was not dead. But no matter how hard Maureen, or I, shook her, she remained obstinately unconscious.

'Let us cover her up,' I said. 'And you, go and fetch her brother. He will want to send for the doctor, I think. This appears much more serious than before.'

Maureen helped me to arrange her mistress's limbs in a seemlier manner, and to pull the top sheet over her naked body. We made no attempt to dress her. The moment Anna was decently covered, Maureen hurried out to find Edwin.

When he came, Edwin stayed only a minute. Horrified to find his dear sister in this sad condition, he rushed back downstairs to send a servant for the doctor. When he returned, he looked distraught. 'If only we lived in town,' he cried. 'In town, we could have a telephone, and have the doctor here so much faster.' He shook his head sadly. 'As it is, it will take at least two hours, provided the servant finds him at home, and there is no delay in bringing him back.'

'I feared something like this,' I told him.

'She was doing so well. I had almost dared to hope that this curse had been lifted.'

There was little we could do but wait. We sat there, Edwin and I, on chairs pulled up beside the bed, mostly in silence. Poor Maureen sat at the dressing table. How must she feel? I wondered. Her mistress was rendered unconscious by some terrible malady and there was naught she could do for her. Even her usual tasks of helping her mistress dress, fussing with her hair, making her day as easy and pleasant as possible, were now stripped from her. Like Edwin, like me, all she could do was wait and hope that the doctor would be able to do something.

It was nearly three hours before we heard the sound of a horse and carriage coming up the long drive. Maureen rushed out, telling Edwin, rather more sternly than she would normally dare to do, to remain by his sister's side, and soon returned with both Doctor Allen and Sir Ulrich.

'She will not awaken,' Edwin declared. 'I don't know what to do.'

Sir Ulrich leaned over the bed, lifting her arm and feeling for a pulse. He pulled out his watch, was quiet for a time, and then let her hand fall to the mattress. 'Only fifty-two beats per minute,' he said.

Behind him, Doctor Allen wrote this in a note-book.

'Were she conscious and resting,' Sir Ulrich said, 'this would be a sign of health. As she is *not* conscious, however, I am concerned. How long has she been like this?'

Edwin looked at me, and I looked at Maureen.

'I came in just at nine o'clock, sir,' Maureen said. 'This is the way I found her. I cannot say how long before that, except that she seemed fine when I helped her prepare for bed last night at half ten.'

'Yes,' I said, 'I can attest to that. She seemed in good health, and good spirits, last night.'

Sir Ulrich bent over Anna and examined her throat with his glass. 'These wounds have not healed,' he stated. 'If anything, they seem fresher than before.' He looked at me, and at Maureen. 'This room has been kept sealed, yes?'

Maureen nodded her agreement. 'It has, Sir Ulrich. And I have been careful to insist that Lady Anna wear the garlic garland about her neck, as you insisted she do.'

'Is it possible she removes it during the night?'

'I could not say,' Maureen replied. 'I do not sleep in her room. And since she has banished Miss Willis to another room, there would be no one here to prevent her doing just that. It was on the pillow when I found her this morning.'

'It must be his influence,' Sir Ulrich said.

'Whose influence?' I asked. Evidently, the men knew something we women did not. How very typical, I thought, that they should exclude those most affected.

'We do not know,' Doctor Allen said.

'We do not even know for sure if it is anyone,' Edwin added. 'We only suspect.'

'May a woman add her suspicions?' I asked. 'Or, her observations, at any rate.'

Sir Ulrich glanced at Maureen. 'Not here,' he said. He looked at his colleague, and at Edwin. 'There is nothing more we can do here. Perhaps we should adjourn to your lordship's library, and Miss Willis can relate her observations. The girl can call us if there is anything new to report.'

'Of course," Edwin said. He rose from his chair. 'Gentlemen, if you will? And, Miss Willis, if you will accompany us, perhaps you may relate something we have so far failed to apprehend. O'Leary, I will send one of the maids in to sit with you. If there is even the slightest change, send her to fetch us at once.'

'As you wish, your lordship.'

I followed the men through the hall, down the main staircase, and towards the back of the house, where Edwin's library was located. It was a large, pleasant room, the walls almost completely covered by built-in book-cases in dark-stained oak. Nearly the only spaces that were not floor-to-ceiling books were above the elaborately-carved mantelpiece, where the floral-patterned green wallpaper surrounded a large oil portrait of the previous earl, above and to either side of the door, and over the two windows, with their deep window seats. The coffered ceiling was bordered by carved cove moulding. A large, ten-mantle gasolier hung from the centre of the ceiling.

Edwin sat behind his desk. Sir Ulrich and Doctor Allen took two of the brown-leather club chairs, and indicated that I should take the third.

'Now,' Sir Ulrich said, 'what is it you wish to tell us? Do you know something that Lady Anna has concealed?'

I nodded. I was still somewhat uncertain as to what I should do. These were things I had learned in the strictest confidence. Were there not a clear danger to my dearest friend's life, I would not have dared to say anything. Now, I felt that I must.

'She has these strange dreams,' I said. 'Sometimes, I feel that I am sharing them with her.'

'What happens in these dreams?'

'First, I am rather embarrassed to say, she throws off her night dress. When she does this her eyes are wide open, yet she is obviously still sleeping. The first time it happened, she was not wearing the garlic, but since then, she removes that as well.'

'What of the cross?' Sir Ulrich asked.

'That remains in place,' I replied.

'Most curious,' the elder physician remarked. 'What happens next?'

'I am afraid there is congress with an unseen lover.'

Doctor Allen had a very curious look on his face. 'Unseen? Is this imaginary, then?'

'From all I can tell, yes. And yet, I rather blush to say this, there does appear to be physical congress taking place.'

'Have you tried to wake her?' Sir Ulrich asked.

'I have never been able to do so. I find myself curiously unable to move when this is happening. If it is a dream, I seem to be a part of it. I cannot think of any other reason I should be frozen in place whilst such outrageous things are happening.'

'I find this very confusing,' Sir Ulrich said. His words seemed to be addressed to the other two men, though I heard them plainly enough. 'The cross, by itself, should have been a sufficient deterrent. And this invisibility? What do we make of this?' He looked back at me:

'Is it possible,' he asked, 'that you were truly awake, but under some enchantment that allowed you to see your friend, but not her spectral lover?'

'I would believe almost anything at the moment,' I admitted.

'Has she said who this phantom lover is?' Doctor Allen asked. 'Has she any idea?'

I nodded my head. 'She is quite sure that it is Lord Ravensbrook.'

'Impossible,' Sir Ulrich declared. He looked at the men. 'You were both with me when we went into the card room, but a few days ago, and clearly saw him reflected in the glass. It cannot be him.'

I looked from one to the other, utterly baffled. 'What are you talking about, gentlemen?' I asked.

'It is time you were told,' Edwin said. 'You are close to my sister, and it may fall to you to watch in what now seem likely to be her final hours. You should know with what we are dealing.'

Conceding Edwin's decision, Sir Ulrich spent several minutes explaining that poor Anna appeared to the victim of a vampire, as well as many of the characteristics of that creature. That he lived by drinking blood; that he was very nearly immortal; that holy things repelled him; that he, being without a soul, cast no reflexion in a mirror.

'That you do not see him is, I think, an aspect of his evil magic. He is there, but he blocks your sight of him, for the old vampire has a powerful mind, and can easily overcome the unprepared,' Sir Ulrich concluded. 'That he leaves the cross, however, this is harder to fathom.'

'I do not understand the mirror test,' I said. 'Has a rock, or a tree, or a table a soul? They reflect perfectly in a mirror. It is not the soul we see, but the physical person. If this is, as poor Anna has said, Lord Ravensbrook, and he has a physical body, why should he not cast a reflexion, whether human or vampire? How much do we truly know about these creatures? Is what we know real, or merely legend and myth?'

'We have also seen him drinking whisky,' Edwin commented.

'I have often eaten or drunk something I did not care for,' I replied, 'because that was what was on offer. If only blood provides nourishment for him, does that mean he cannot drink other things that do not? Is whisky poisonous to a vampire? Is wine?'

'The young lady makes valid points,' Sir Ulrich declared, after taking some minutes to think it all over. 'I will admit that the cross confuses me, but we do know that he will not venture out into the sunlight, and that is supposedly an infallible sign.'

'Perhaps this is a foolish question,' I said, 'but do you know how old this vampire is?'

'No, we do not.'

'When he first appeared in these parts, Lady Anna and I made a point of looking Lord Ravensbrook up in Burke's. The title dates from the reign of Henry VII, and there seems to be an odd tradition in the family of always naming the eldest son Anthony. In truth, there was nothing to indicate that any generation has produced more than one child. Is it not possible that we are not, in fact, dealing with the fifteenth Lord Ravensbrook, but with the first and only? If so, he would be more than four hundred years old, and very likely have been a Catholic in life. The cross around Lady Anna's neck is a plain one. Perhaps he is only repelled by a crucifix, but not a plain cross.'

'I think,' Sir Ulrich said to Edwin, 'that it is time we paid a visit to your neighbour.'

'We should have one less barrier if we go now,' Doctor Allen said. 'As we were arriving here, I noticed his butler just starting towards the village.'

'Then you should find his lordship alone,' I said. 'I have been told he has but the one servant in the house.'

'Then we shall go at once,' Edwin declared. He turned to me. 'You will, of course, remain here. Keep watch over Anna, like the dear friend that you are.'

'Of course.'

I took my leave of the men and returned to Anna's room. Nothing had changed, save that Olive, one of the chamber maids, had joined the vigil at Anna's bedside. Now that I had returned, the girl was dismissed to return to her normal duties.

I feared this would be a long vigil.

XXXIII: Lord Muntglare's Journal

Tuesday, 30th July— Miss Willis's words had a galvanising effect upon the three of us. Though she might have some doubts, we three knew full well that vampires were real. Within a quarter hour of her returning to her vigil in my sister's room, we had prepared for our foray. Doctor Allen had his revolver in his pocket. I had my sword-stick, and Sir Ulrich had his medical bag, which, in addition to the usual tools of his profession, contained a sharpened wooden stake and a heavy hammer.

As we did not wish our visit to become public knowledge, we walked across the estate and climbed over the wall that separates my property from Lord Ravensbrook's. It was not too likely that anyone would have noticed had we gone around in the phaeton, for the road is not heavily travelled, yet the extra precaution seemed warranted. If the marquess proved to be the vampire we sought, then we meant to destroy him. In these modern times, people do not believe in vampires. Particularly in England, where there has never been the superstitious attachment to the occult that predominates in the Balkans and the more remote regions of eastern Europe, and in which the vampire figures prominently.

Nay, here we know only the literary vampire. Varney, Lord Ruthven, the Countess Karnstein, and a few others. Characters in fiction, meant to entertain, not physical monsters preying upon living people. If we destroy the vampire, it is certainly possible that the police will not recognise this as a public service, but treat it as a murder. It would be for the best, therefore, if no one outside our little circle knew what had happened.

Lord Ravensbrook's butler was still away, and we pounded upon the door to no avail. Either the marquess was away, or he was not answering the door. 'Very likely, he is resting in his coffin,' Sir Ulrich opined. 'It would be best if we discover him thus, for that would provide the proof we need.'

'How shall we enter?' Doctor Allen enquired.

'Let us try the obvious first,' I replied, taking hold of the door handle and pressing down on the latch. I had seen too many plays in which the comic hero is stymied because he didn't think to check whether a door was locked to make the same mistake myself. The test was to no avail. The door was locked.

'Let us go around the house,' I said. 'Perhaps there is an unlatched window.'

Our survey proved fruitful. There was a partially-opened window in the kitchen, and we clambered through it.

A quick survey of our surroundings suggested that we might be on the right track. The kitchen was large, intended to serve both a family and all of their retainers, yet it seemed little used. If Lord Ravensbrook was, indeed, the vampire we thought him to be, it was likely that only his butler made use of the kitchen. The marquess would find his nourishment elsewhere.

For safety's sake, we decided to search the house together. It would, no doubt, have been more efficient to split up, but what if we encountered the vampire? In that event, there was safety in numbers. We knew this from our encounter with the late Miss Cooper. Even a young vampire, it seemed, was much stronger than a mortal, so how much stronger would an ancient master vampire be? If Lord Ravensbrook is as old as Miss Willis suggests, he must be powerful indeed.

Searching the servants' quarters confirmed our suspicion. Only one room showed signs of occupancy. All the others were furnished, but it was clear the beds were not slept on, and there was no clothing, nor any other personal belongings in any of them.

We found a similar aura of dis-use in the rest of the house. The bedrooms were furnished in an old-fashioned style that seemed nearly contemporary with the oldest parts of the building, yet the beds seemed unused, and there was nothing to set one room apart from another. They had the sterile uniformity of an hotel.

We went through the entire house in a systematic manner, but there was no one to be found. If Lord Ravensbrook was present, he was also well-hidden. After over an hour of searching, we exited as we had entered, through the kitchen window. We had been careful not to disturb anything, so we could reasonably hope that, when the butler returned, he would find nothing amiss and our visit would remain a secret.

Still, it was a despondent crew that returned to the New Lodge this day. Though we seemed to have further proof that my neighbour was not what he seemed, we had no more idea than when we had started out of how to conclusively prove this, nor of where he might be hidden in that ancient house.

'Perhaps there is an old priest's hole,' Doctor Allen suggested. 'The house is of the right period for such a thing.'

'It is not, in fact,' I replied. 'Winstead only dates from the Protectorate, though I suppose it entirely possible that a hidden room was installed for other purposes. As a repository for treasure, perhaps? The problem, should that be true, is how do we discover its location? Other than to-day, I have not been inside that house since I was a small child, and I was never shown any priest's holes, or hidden passageways, or any of the secret hiding places that the writers of popular romantic tales are wont to employ. I would not discount the idea that they exist, but I have no idea of where they might be concealed.'

We were then interrupted by a gentle rapping at the door. I called for whoever it was to enter, and the door opened to disclose O'Leary, my sister's lady's maid. 'What is it?' I asked.

'Your sister is awake, your lordship,' she said. 'Miss Willis asked me to inform you.'

XXXIV: Doctor Allen's Journal

Wednesday, 31st July— No journal yesterday, so I shall attempt to catch up to-day. We were summoned to Muntglare shortly after eleven o'clock in the morning. Or, perhaps more accurately, I was summoned. Lord Muntglare would not have been aware of Sir Ulrich's return to High Coulston early that morning, or that he would be available to accompany me and offer his learned insights.

The message brought by the groom was straightforward enough. Lady Anna could not be wakened. We set out at once, pausing only to collect our bags, and a few necessary items. Sir Ulrich added a sharpened wooden stake and heavy hammer to his bag. I pocketed my revolver. If a crisis had been reached for Lady Anna, the odds seemed very strong that we should again embark upon a vampire hunt.

If we could determine who the vampire was.

Poor Miss Cooper was now thoroughly and finally dead, her headless body, which we could not return to its grave, now laid to rest in a noble tomb. She would never harm anyone again. It was the master vampire, the fiend who had laid that demonic curse of the un-dead upon the poor girl, whom we now must seek out and destroy.

Lady Anna we found in her boudoir, unconscious and unable to respond to anything we could decently do to stimulate a response. She appeared to be in no particular distress, save her comatose condition.

Miss Willis was able to enlighten us on the strange nocturnal visitations the poor woman has suffered these past weeks. Sir Ulrich declared that the "imaginary" visitor was quite real, and that he was invisible to Miss Willis through some mystical glamour that allowed her to see his actions, but not to see him. Sir Ulrich noted that the wounds on Lady Anna's neck appear fresh, which suggests to him that our vampire was active during the night leading up to this state.

Miss Willis also suggested a flaw in Professor von Elbing's methodology for identifying a vampire. If the vampire was corporeal, and not merely a manifestation of an invisible spectre, she argued that the vampire *must* cast a reflexion in a looking glass, just as any other physical object, whether possessed of a soul or not.

As Lady Anna identified her nocturnal visitor, whom she believed to be a part of a particularly vivid dream, as Lord Ravensbrook, Lord Muntglare, Sir Ulrich, and I made up an expedition and searched his house whilst his butler, now known to be his only retainer, was away in the village. We found evidence that Lord Ravensbrook lives alone, but we did not find the lord himself. Sir Ulrich suspects a hidden room, a priest's hole, or something of the like, where he has concealed his coffin, and to which he resorts during the day.

Shortly after we returned from our expedition, Lady Anna's servant, O'Leary, informed us that her mistress was now awake. We rushed to her room, and found her sitting up in her bed, propped up on a stack of pillows, looking rather pale.

She confessed that she had no idea what had happened. When Sir Ulrich mentioned that we now knew about her 'dreams,' and that Miss Willis had revealed the entire story, 'for she was in fear for your life, and neither modesty nor propriety can be more important than life,' she admitted as much, and that she had been subjected to a similar visitation the previous night.

'You must not remain alone at night,' Sir Ulrich said. 'It is clear that we are dealing with a vampire now, and it is also clear that he is able to come and go as he wishes. Perhaps, this is another of the accepted "facts" that are not true. It is said that no vampire can enter a home unless invited in.'

'Which means nothing here,' Lord Muntglare pointed out, 'as the suspected individual has been our guest in this house many times.'

'True. Once invited in, the vampire may come and go as he pleases.'

'I fear having company during the night, Sir Ulrich,' Lady Anna said. 'The reason I asked Miss Willis to sleep in another room was that I was experiencing an overwhelming compulsion to, I fear to say, bite her. Is that the vampire curse working within me?'

'I fear it is, dear lady. And, as the affliction grows stronger, so will these strange desires. You may start to crave blood, for instance.'

'I do now,' Lady Anna admitted. 'I am ravenously hungry, and the thing I most desire is a steak, only lightly cooked, so that the blood still oozes from the pink flesh.'

'No, Lady Anna, I do not think this would be a good idea.' Sir Ulrich looked meaningfully at her brother. 'I must recommend a meatless diet for Lady Anna, at least, until we have found the cause of her distress and dealt with it.'

'I will so inform the kitchen staff,' Lord Muntglare said.

To-day— We remained at Muntglare through the night. In accordance with Sir Ulrich's instructions, Miss Willis and O'Leary stayed in Lady Anna's room while she slept. This cannot have been easy for either of them. Miss Willis is one of Lady Anna's closest friends, and O'Leary has been with her for several years. Now, they must watch her by night, lest she suffer yet another attack. She grows weaker with each assault, and we physicians have no obvious cure for the malady that afflicts her. We have some power to cure physical ailments, to be sure, and each year brings more and better weapons and knowledge to our fight, but this is a *meta*physical assault.

Miss Willis informed us that the night passed without incident. Lady Anna seems stronger to-day. She is out of bed, and trying to resume her usual activities, though at a reduced pace. She seems somewhat at a loss without the assistance of the faithful O'Leary, who was sent to bed once she had dressed her mistress. So, too, was Miss Willis. Neither of these staunch young women has slept since rising yesterday morning, and, as they will watch to-night as well, both are greatly in need of restorative rest.

Sir Ulrich seems to have cornered the garlic market in High Coulston. He has thoroughly sealed up the windows and hearth in Lady Anna's room, so that, even should he assume the form of a miasmic emanation, the garlic around the edges of the windows should frustrate our vampire in his efforts to enter. It does not, of course, improve the atmosphere in the room, which now reeks of the Mediterranean staple. I do not care for it. I prefer to eat much the same diet as my ancestors, though, as a physician, I am able to purchase better quality than they could when I was a child in London's East End. In those days, my rather inadequate diet was a side effect of my father's obsession with seeing that his eldest son would receive a university education. That education is why, in their old age, my parents live in a semi-fashionable suburb, rather than in the old terraced house I grew up in.

I find myself thinking of how nice it would be if Lord Muntglare possessed a telephone. It is such a great convenience for a doctor. Without there being one here — which, his lordship tells me, there will not be for at least another five years — I am reliant upon my patients having to send a messenger out to Muntglare should there be an emergency back in the village. Like Sir Ulrich, I am uncomfortable leaving our patient without immediate medical aid.

A strange article in to-day's Record, which I shall insert here. I am forced to wonder if Lord Ravensbrook, and poor Miss Cooper, are the only threats to this region:

STRANGE ANIMAL MUTILATION
DEAD SHEEP DISCOVERED
HIGH COULSTON HORROR RETURNS?

31st July — Farmer John Turling, whose holdings are upon the north-eastern border of the village, contacted the police early this morning after finding one of his prize Merino sheep dead from an apparent animal attack. The police have indicated that the animal was killed by a single bite to the throat, and that the carcass appears to have been drained of blood, but otherwise unconsumed.

Some of farmer Turling's neighbours have raised the possibility that the so-called 'High Coulston Horror,' the unknown animal responsible for the death of Alice Milton, may be responsible. Police are no closer to finding that animal now than on the day of the first outrage. When asked about this, Inspector Royce replied only that they were 'looking into' any possible connexions. Farmer Turling

> would only comment that, if it was the same animal,
> he would have to concede that it was better to lose
> a sheep than another person, but, all the same, he
> would rather lose neither.

I could not avoid noticing the similarity. On the other hand, it struck me that this was an attack on an animal, whilst Sir Ulrich's sources declare that vampires only prey upon human beings. Still, his little book seems to have been wrong about looking glasses and, perhaps, crosses, so perhaps it is wrong about this as well. Were he otherwise conformable to society, I suppose a vampire might be tolerable if he obtained his diet from the slaughter-man, and not from the throats of unwilling victims.

Well, that hardly matters, does it? The vampire we are pursuing most certainly *does* get his nourishment from the throats of unwilling human victims. Worse, he turns his victims into creatures like himself, so that this plague must inevitably spread.

I shall have to return home to-day. I cannot leave my surgery unattended for too long, lest I return to find some poor soul dead who I might have saved had I been there. Sir Ulrich will stay here at Muntglare for now.

XXXV: Maureen O'Leary's Diary

Thursday, 1st August— Another night of watching over my poor mistress. It is terribly oppressive in her room, with the reek of garlic from where Sir Ulric has placed cloves of the horrible stuff around the window frames and the hearth. Fortunately, I watch with Suzanne, and we are able to allow each other a few minutes in each hour to leave the room and breathe the sweeter air in the corridor.

I fear that my mistress is succumbing to her illness. I am not certain that I fully understand what is happening. I have, to be sure, read of vampires. LeFanu's *Carmilla* is amongst the books I keep in my room, as is Polidori's *The Vampyre*. If, as dear Suzanne says the men believe, it is Lord Ravensbrook who is the vampire, there would seem to me to be an obvious connexion with the latter book. Polidori's Lord Ruthven is said to be young, handsome, and quite charming, though also concealing a heart of the purest, most selfish evil. Lord Ravensbrook is certainly young and charming, and quite well-spoken, or so I have been told. I have not had occasion to speak to him myself, though I have seen him at times when he has visited the house. If he is evil as well, then the parallel is complete.

I must admit that I prefer LeFanu's work to Polidori's. *The Vampyre* is little more than a short story, with its silly paean to Lord Byron wrapped around it. One must, to be sure, feel some pity for Polidori himself, for he seemed greatly in awe of his patron, but also greatly damaged by his association. I am sure it did not help when what he considered his greatest work was attributed, in the popular mind and press, to Byron, despite the protests of *both* men. Polidori complained that credit was taken from him and given to another; Byron, by many accounts, complained about precisely the opposite, that he was being credited for what he considered an inferior work. I do not doubt that both Byron's rejection of himself and his work, and the ridicule heaped upon poor Polidori, both contributed to him taking his own life.

The story of the beautiful young Laura and the alluring vampire, Carmilla, is, I think, a superior work. It has the necessary elements of suspense and adventure, along with a ruthless, ancient villainess, who is yet at least somewhat sympathetic. It is clear enough that Carmilla, or Mircalla, to give her the name she bore when she was still the living Countess Karnstein, is enamoured of Laura. To what extent this love is returned, LeFanu's insistence upon clinging to the moral codes of Ireland makes unclear. It is surely true that two women may love each other with a love as pure and sweet as the love between any man and woman. Perhaps purer and sweeter, for such love does not inevitably descend to the terrible, commercial finale of marriage, wherein the poor bride is forced to give up so much of what makes her a unique person, turning her fate over to a man who may, in truth, not be up to the challenge.

Turning over her fortune, too. Just as I would not wish to become the virtual slave of any man, so would I quail at handing over control of my bank account to any of the uneducated labourers my mother constantly proffers as potential mates. I have nearly enough on deposit to purchase a comfortable cottage in the village, and between the three books I currently have in print, another due to go on sale in September, and one more half-completed, I expect to have more than enough to not only buy the cottage, but to live in it in some degree of comfort. Why should I give this to some lout who will only throw it away in the pub?

If I must ultimately marry, let him at least be a gentleman.

My mistress seemed to become agitated just as the hall clock was striking two o'clock. I did not see any cause for this, nor did Suzanne, who had also noticed that something was happening to her friend.

Writhing about in her sleep, Lady Anna pushed the sheet off her sleeping form. With her eyes still shut, she clawed up the hem of her night dress. Her right hand began to violently caress her quim, and soon she was moaning with pleasure.

'Is this the vampire, then?' I whispered.

'No,' replied Suzanne. 'This is something different. Now she is pleasuring herself, and before her arms were wrapped around an unseen lover, and you could see her lovely cunt open and stretch, as if accommodating an invisible member.'

'Should we intervene?'

Suzanne shook her head. 'I do not think so. Perhaps this is her body's way of gaining a more natural release after being subjected to the vampire's enforced carnality.'

'I must say, sitting here watching this is having an effect on my own carnality,' I admitted.

She looked at me and smiled. 'Perhaps,' she said, 'when our watch is over, before you go to your bed, you might visit me in my room and help me to, uhm, to undress.'

'I would be happy to assist you, my dear Miss Willis,' I said.

Sir Ulrich and Lord Muntglare rapped upon the door at seven o'clock. By this time, my mistress was sleeping again, and we had re-arranged her night dress and pulled the sheets back over her. She seemed none the worse for her nocturnal self-abuse — a term I really do not care for, as it suggests there is something wrong in sexual pleasure.

Now, it is true, the practice is said to cause all manner of ill effects in men, including insanity, blindness, and moral degeneracy. Yet, if it were truly harmful in a woman, why, then, do physicians spend so much time and effort treating so many female conditions by fingering their female patients' cunts until they climax?

Having turned the care of my sleeping mistress over to the elderly physician and her brother, I followed Suzanne across the corridor to her room. I was done with work until the evening, when I would again keep watch. If my mistress decided to get out of bed and dress, one of the other maids would assist her.

As soon as we were inside her room, and the door safely locked, Suzanne began to undress. She favours styles that do not require the assistance of a lady's maid, but, naturally, I knew this before coming her with her. That it was all a pretence.

'I fear I am abusing you, dear Maureen,' she said, placing her waistcoat on a chair and starting to undo the buttons of her shirtwaist. 'But seeing my darling during the night, watching her writhing with erotic abandon, and knowing that I cannot be with her so long as this strange malady afflicts her, I *need* to be with someone.'

I had hung my apron over the back of the same chair and was slowly releasing the buttons on my bodice. 'I feel the same needs,' I said. 'Sometimes, physical satisfaction is all that is desired, and, if the desire be mutual, it will suffice.'

Very soon, we were both stark naked. Remembering what happened the first time, Suzanne had closed the draperies *before* we started undressing. We stood almost toe to toe, facing each other, me looking slightly upward to gaze into those emerald eyes. I am only an inch above five feet tall, but I need look upward but little, as Suzanne is no more than an inch taller than me. I adore those eyes, and that coppery-red hair that now, loosened, was falling down her back, and across her white shoulders and lovely, firm breasts.

It struck me as mildly ironic that here she was, as thoroughly English as someone could be, with green eyes and red hair, and here I was, Irish born, of a family with ancient, if common, roots in that beleaguered country, with brown eyes and brown hair. I had no doubt, were someone to see the two of us, and be tasked with guessing where each was from, unless he heard us speak he would reverse the heritage.

I pushed her back, so that she sat on the edge of the bed, and knelt in front of her. Spreading her legs, I leaned forward, my nose nuzzling in the brilliant red thatch, my fingers carefully parting her lips, so that her pearl of all pleasure peeked out and presented itself to my wet tongue. She sighed, her body shivering as I licked. My fingers slid smoothly into her secret sheath, loving the slick, roughly-smooth depths.

Her fingers stroked my hair, pulling me tighter against her quivering blossom. Already, I could feel her body beginning to stretch and tighten. She made soft, whimpering sounds, her breath becoming ragged, catching in her throat. Closer and closer she came, until her whole body convulsed with passion and she collapsed back onto the bed, exhausted.

This would be for her, I thought. Already, she was falling asleep, naked, her body lying across her bed, her legs hanging over the side. Gently, I helped her arrange herself for sleep, pulling back the covers, getting her under them. She was still naked, but she would be decently covered as she slept.

When Suzanne was settled in her bed, I quickly redressed myself, slipped out of her room, and made my way back to the servants' quarters and my own room. I spent some few minutes conversing with Mrs Irving, who was naturally curious about our patient. Then, quite exhausted, I retired to my room, undressed again, and climbed into my bed.

XXXVI: Doctor Heilger's *Tagebuch*

***Thursday, 1st August*—** I am more and more worried about my beautiful young patient. The signs are appearing. She continues to wear the cross, which tells me she is not yet too far gone. At the same time, I believe that I can see her upper canine teeth growing sharper, though they have not yet begun to lengthen. At what point, then, does the transformation become inevitable? When is the sweet, gentle lady irrevocably replaced by the evil, blood-sucking monster? When does the chaste and honourable give way to the lascivious seductress?

There are stories from olden times, brought down over the centuries in eastern Europe and the Balkans, of the seductive nature of the vampire. The tale of the heroic Magyar knight, Bela of Szerencs, who, after many adventures, found the vampire, Szonja, resting in her coffin in a deep crypt. Yet, though he should have destroyed her upon the instant, he was so fascinated by her unnatural beauty that he stood in rapt adoration until the sun had fled the sky, and she awoke and took his life, and made a vampire of him.

Surely, we have seen exactly this sort of mesmeric fascination in Doctor Allen's pitying regret at the destruction of the vampire animating the poor Cooper girl. One cannot 'reform' a vampire, beautiful though she may be.

One may pity the creature, to be sure, for how often would any sane person seek out such a fate? Even the oldest of vampires was, at the beginning, the victim of another.

We must destroy the master vampire. It is the only hope for poor Lady Anna. Or, I believe this to be so. Yet we have seen other long-held beliefs shattered. The mirror test, the repulsive power of the holy. I fear this will be another, that the destruction of the master vampire may not break the curse on the victim, and she will inevitably transform and must be destroyed in her turn. We can only know after we have destroyed the master, and there is no surety that this will be done before poor Lady Anna has passed beyond recovery.

We know who he is. We even know where he dwells. Somewhere, within that ancient house at Winstead, the monster keeps his lair.

XXXVII: Suzanne Willis's Diary

Friday, 2nd August— Last night was the crisis, or so I believe. Maureen and I again kept watch over Anna during the night. There has not been a true attack in a week, yet she continues to grow weaker, save only the brief recovery at the time of our outing. I do not know what to do, and this vexes me. My dearest friend, my favourite lover, is slowly dying.

Dear Maureen is a comfort, but while she provides me with physical relief, and is a lovely, caring young woman, she is not Anna. There is something deeper there, something that will certainly remain even after we are old, married women, as we must eventually become. Or as I must become. I fear that Anna will not survive this continuing attack.

Curiously, though we know who the monster is, there is naught we can do through any normal means. Should anyone attempt to involve the police, the only result would be a trip to Bedlam, for vampires are not within the constabulary's purview. I would hardly believe it myself, had I not seen what was happening. Even if I could not see Lord Ravensbrook there, I knew it was he from what Anna, who evidently *could* see him, told me.

We sat quietly in that gloomy room, breathing in the garlic-tainted air. Were it left to me, I should remove every clove and every flower, but Sir Ulrich insists that this is necessary, that it protects my darling from the monster.

Maureen was reading, *Les Misérables,* untranslated. She is an intriguing girl. I know she comes from quite a common background, and no one who ever heard her speak could doubt that she was Irish. Yet, though she speaks with a thick brogue, her grammar is that of an educated woman, and, obviously, she at least *reads* French.

'Is it better in French?' I asked. 'I have only read that in translation, and found it rather tedious.'

Maureen looked up from her book and smiled. 'I believe novels are always better in the original language,' she replied. 'However, even in his own tongue, Hugo never uses one word if he can find a way to use ten or twenty instead.'

We lapsed into silence again. In the hall, the clock struck the hour and half-hour with tardy regularity. Time passed so slowly that it seemed hardly to pass at all. Anna slept, and Maureen read, and I suppose one could say that I fretted and worried.

The clock had just struck three when I noticed a dense mist stealing under the corridor door. I started to alert Maureen, but realised I could not move. Glancing over at the girl, it was obvious she had been deprived of movement as well, for she sat there with a page half turned, frozen in the act.

The mist pooled beside the bed, rising up into a nebulous column before disappearing from view. Presumably, it had now taken the form of Lord Ravensbrook, though to me it was as invisible as ever it had been before.

And there was Anna, throwing off her night dress and tossing the garlic garland across the bed and onto the floor. Her arms were upraised, welcoming, and she drew up her legs, soon wrapping both arms and legs about her invisible lover. She arched her back, her slender neck stretching backwards, and I could see the two little marks growing red as the blood flowed into a phantom mouth.

Somehow, I am not sure how, I managed a little movement. Only a little, but it was enough to knock the little silver bell off the small table that sat between Maureen and me. It made a remarkable clang, for it struck the table leg in falling.

That sudden noise seemed to break the spell, for suddenly we both could move again. Maureen shrieked to wake the dead. I had no weapon, but I threw myself onto my writhing lover and was shocked to find that, though I could not *see* her attacker, he was palpable.

The door burst open, and Lord Muntglare rushed in, brandishing a wicked-looking naval hanger. Sir Ulrich and Doctor Allen, who had returned during the late afternoon, followed him into the room.

It was at that point that all doubt was dispelled. Perhaps the vampire simply could not maintain the illusion of invisibility before so many. Perhaps it was merely the presence of three who had not been subjected to the original spell. Whatever the cause, we were suddenly confronted by Lord Ravensbrook himself.

This was not the noble gentlemen who had so often graced our parlour over recent weeks. No, this was a monster. There was a trickle of blood running from his lips. He stood there, defiant, anger etched upon his usually handsome face. He was naked, and I realised that the slim figure I had so admired when he was in evening dress was something of an illusion, for he had the body of an immensely powerful, hard-muscled man.

'Now we have you!' Edwin declared.

'Ha!' the marquess shouted, defiantly. 'What do you think that you can do? To me? You are infants compared to me. Have *you* ever seen battle? Were *you* there at Bosworth? Did *your* sword pierce the brain of a king? You are nothing to me.'

The men rushed at him, but in the instant, he dissolved into that insubstantial mist and flowed out through the door.

'I feel the perfect fool,' Sir Ulrich declared, watching the mist trail away. 'I blocked all the windows, I blocked the hearth, yet somehow it never occurred to me that he could enter anywhere in the house.'

'What can we do now?' Doctor Allen asked.

The elder physician looked at him, then at the poor figure on the bed. 'Until the sun is up, we can do nothing. For now, let us tend to this poor lady.'

They did what they could, but that was precious little. Though there was the physical injury from the loss of blood, the danger was predominantly metaphysical. We got poor Anna back into her night dress, and decently covered her with the sheet, but she had again lapsed into that comatose state she had languished under before.

At length, the men departed to make their plans, leaving me with Maureen to watch over poor Anna.

XXXVIII: Lord Muntglare's Journal

Friday, 2nd August— The physicians having done all that they could for Anna, we retired to my library to make our plans. Now there was no question. We had seen Lord Ravensbrook in the very act of sating his vampiric lust on my innocent sister. We also knew that we were dealing with a very old, very powerful vampire. 'My strength is as the strength of ten, because my heart is pure.' So said Tennyson. It seems that the vampire's strength may be quite as great, but not from any purity of heart. No, the monster gains his strength by stealing it from his victims.

'We must make our assault the moment the sun has risen," Sir Ulrich insisted. 'There has to be some hidden place in that old house where he is hiding. If we can find it during daylight hours, he will be powerless, and a stake through the heart will put him finally in his grave for good and all.'

'What of the butler?' Doctor Allen enquired.

'He is elderly,' I replied. 'He will cause us no great inconvenience.'

'Perhaps,' Sir Ulrich said, 'he can be persuaded to assist us. He will be loyal, but how many men remain loyal at the risk of death? If he has been protecting this monster, then he is as guilty of these depredations as his master.'

'We can threaten,' I said, 'but, so long as he is a man and not himself a vampire, he will know that his life is in no great danger. Threatening to kill someone for information is a useless gesture, for only a complete fool would fail to recognise that you need your subject alive if he is to reveal the information.'

We gathered our equipment and made our plans. Doctor Allen had his revolver. We knew it would be useless against a vampire, but it might well serve to intimidate a human servant. I would again have my sword-stick. Sir Ulrich was armed with his stake and hammer. He also carried a large crucifix and a bottle of holy water. 'Both blessed by a *Catholic* priest,' he told us. 'In case Miss Willis was correct in her supposition.'

We found ourselves climbing over the wall dividing the properties just as the first hint of dawn coloured the eastern sky. The sun had appeared by the time we reached the house. Doctor Allen hammered at the door, and after a long time it was opened by the ancient butler.

'We must see your master at once,' Sir Ulrich declared.

'He is not here.'

'We know that he is,' I interjected. 'Now, let us enter.'

'That, I may not do,' the butler answered.

'I think you will,' Doctor Allen said, taking his revolver from his pocket.

The butler instinctively backed away and we pushed our way into the house.

Once again, we searched the entire house, and, once again, we found nothing. The butler followed up closely, but made no attempt to hinder us. I imagine he was confident that we would not be able to find his master's hidden lair. After searching for an hour, I was starting to think that he was correct.

We had searched the library first and found nothing. Now we returned to that room. As it happened, the light from the rising sun shone through a window in the eastern wall, its rays shining obliquely across the geometric patterns of the carpet. Now I could see what had been invisible before. There was a slight arc in the nap of the carpet, as if something had been repeatedly swung across it at that point. This exactly corresponded to the placement of one of the tall, built-in book cases.

'A secret door,' I said, excitedly.

We at once set about gaining entrance. Pulling availed us nothing. We began removing books, thinking that perhaps a false volume served as the latch. It was as we were doing this that I accidentally kicked against the trim at the bottom of the book case. It seemed to me that I felt it give slightly, so I pressed hard against it with my foot. There was a sharp, metallic click, and one side of the book case moved outward perhaps a quarter of an inch.

Now, when we pulled on that side, the whole book case swung out, revealing an unframed opening in the wall, with a staircase beyond leading down.

In our excitement, we had forgotten the butler. He came at us with a letter knife, but between us we disarmed him. 'We must ensure he does not interfere,' Sir Ulrich said. He opened his bag and produced a length of stout rope. 'Let us tie him to a chair.'

It was a matter of a minute or so to secure the butler. Then, taking lamps from the library, we began to descend the hidden staircase. Down it led, deeper and deeper into the foundation of the old house. At the bottom, we found what we were looking for. A heavy oaken door barred our entry into whatever was beyond.

Sir Ulrich, it seemed, included lock picking amongst his skills. It took him perhaps ten minutes to defeat the lock, and to spring back the bolt. With a feeling of triumph, we pulled open the massive door.

Beyond it was a square, windowless, stone room, perhaps eight feet to the side. The massive construction, and the thick door, made me suspect I had been right. This room had been constructed to guard treasure. Now, on a low platform, it sheltered only an oaken coffin.

Sir Ulrich produced his stake and hammer, wishing to be ready to act the moment the lid was opened. In the event, such hasty action was unneeded. When we lifted the coffin lid, its occupant was lying there at rest, eyes closed, seemingly dead.

'We do this for God,' Sir Ulrich said, placing the point of the stake over the vampire's heart. 'And for your dear sister.'

He raised the hammer and brought it down in a mighty blow. Vulcan himself could not have struck with greater force. The slender stake, sharpened to a needle point, transfixed the vampire's body in a single blow.

We leapt back as Lord Ravensbrook writhed in the coffin, blood spraying from the fatal wound. After a minute he lay still. After two minutes, his body began to desiccate and shrivel. Death, delayed some four centuries, was asserting itself. Within half an hour, the corpse had fallen away into elemental dust, leaving only the dried bones, still dressed in a fine suit, within the coffin.

Sir Ulrich hacked off the head and placed it between the skeleton's feet. He sprinkled the holy water throughout the coffin, and placed the crucifix upon the breast, next to the protruding stake. As the lid would not close, he took a surgical saw from his bag and cut off the upper part of the stake, leaving the rest where it was. The lid was closed, more holy water sprinkled, and we departed the crypt and returned to the library.

The butler, it seemed, had not long survived his master. His body sagged in its bonds. The two physicians untied him, and laid him on the carpet. In death, he looked years older than he had in life. I wondered if his master had found a way to prolong his servant's life as a reward for keeping him safe over the years, and now that his master was dead, that protection vanished, and nature caught up with the fellow.

We took the butler's body back to his room and laid it on the bed. When he was found, as he certainly would be eventually, there was every chance the coroner would conclude that he simply died there. As Doctor Allen would naturally be called upon to perform any post mortem, the result was a foregone conclusion.

Returning to the library, we closed the book case. That would do for the moment. We decided that we would return after we had checked on Anna, bringing bricks, mortar, and plaster, and seal up the opening behind the book case, so that if it were to be opened at some time in the future all that would be revealed was a blank wall.

XXXIX: Suzanne Willis's Diary

Friday, 2nd August— It was the strangest thing. At precisely three minutes after eight o'clock this morning, my darling Anna suddenly sat up in bed. She looked around the room, wrinkled her pretty nose at the garlic odour, and gazed over at me. Her expression was one of surprise.

'Why are you sitting there?' she asked. 'And, O'Leary, you, too? Why do you both look so grave, so shocked?'

As I watched, the marks on her throat began to fade. In a few minutes, they were gone, and the colour had returned to her cheeks. One moment she was hovering near death, and now she seemed entirely restored to her old self.

At that moment, I realised, the vampire had been destroyed. Sir Ulrich and his books had been wrong about certain things, but it appeared that they had been correct in this. With her master dead, the connexion was broken, and his victim instantly restored. If one is to believe miracles are still possible in this modern age, Anna's swift recovery surely qualifies.

By the time the men returned, Anna had dressed. Oh, it was a joyous reunion of brother and sister, for I knew poor Edwin had all too seriously questioned whether his goal could be accomplished, and his sister brought back from the brink of death. Yet here she was, as vivacious as ever a young lady of her age should be.

Though it was still early in the day, Edwin had several bottles of excellent wine brought up from his cellars. Edwin, Sir Ulrich, and Anna had some of the Bordeaux, whilst Doctor Allen and I sampled the Riesling. Even dear Maureen was included in the celebration, though, as a servant, this would not have been the usual thing. Because of her role in caring for Anna during her illness, she was privy to everything, and had seen the vampire with her own eyes. It seemed only fair to include her as we celebrated, even to afford her the status of almost a social equal as we celebrated, though, naturally, her status reverted to normal immediately after.

'I must say, I had my doubts we could accomplish this thing,' Edwin declared. 'It was nothing more than pure chance we even discovered the monster's lair. Had the sun risen only a little higher in the eastern sky, I doubt we should have noticed the marks on the carpet that led to the secret room.'

'I suspect we would have found it,' Sir Ulrich said. 'Surely you noticed that the butler became more agitated when we entered the library? This told me that we were in the proper room. The only question then became, where is the door hidden? It might have taken us somewhat longer, but I am sure we would have found it.'

'Fortunately, we did not have to rely upon such a diligent examination of the room," Doctor Allen said. 'The rising sun lit the way. Ironic, is it not? The vampire fears the sunlight, and it was the sunlight that disclosed his lair.'

'We must seal that lair for all time,' Edwin declared. 'There are bricks and mortar stored in the stables. Plaster, too, if I remember correctly. The estate will no doubt come on the market again at some future date, and it would obviously be best to leave no trace of that old strong room for a new owner to discover.'

Doctor Allen pulled his watch from his waistcoat pocket. 'I fear I must make an early departure,' he said. 'I have a patient who needs my attention. Not so interesting as our recent adventure, to be sure, but this is what I do.' He looked at Edwin. 'May I beg the favour that you might provide transport for Sir Ulrich to the station, your lordship? I presume he may wish to remain here a while longer.'

Edwin nodded. 'Of course.' He glanced at Sir Ulrich. 'Will you need to return to the doctor's home, or may we deliver you directly to the station when the times arrives?'

'My traps are here,' Sir Ulrich said. 'The station will be fine. It is, indeed, time for me to return to London. There are medical students there who will need my guidance very soon.'

'There is a nine o'clock train for London this evening,' Edwin reported, after checking the time-table. 'I will have Jackson take you in the phaeton in plenty of time.'

'Excellent. Thank you, your lordship.'

Doctor Allen departed a few minutes later. Sir Ulrich set off for the station after supper. I found I was looking forward to the night, for this would be the first time in several days when it would be possible for me to resume my place beside dear Anna in her bed.

XL: Doctor Allen's Journal

Friday, 2nd August— It was a great relief when Sir Ulrich determined to travel directly from Muntglare to the station. My household is in some degree of disorder just now. The redoubtable Mrs Dumphy has returned to Scotland to care for her elderly mother. I find it difficult to imagine how ancient that old lady must be, for Mrs Dumphy was sixty-three on her last birthday, and, she has told me, was the *youngest* of nine children.

Well, George, are you fooling yourself as you write this? It is not whatever small disorder may have been caused by the housekeeper's departure that found you wishing Sir Ulrich would not return to your home, was it? No, there is a more tender reason for that wish.

I must admit, I was surprised when his plan for the destruction of Lord Ravensbrook bore fruit. His record as a vampire expert, after all, seems rather clouded. He was wrong about mirrors, wrong about crosses and other holy things and, I think, only partially right about garlic. But, it seems, he was right about staking a vampire through the heart. Lord Ravensbrook will not revive. His body has fallen to dust. His influence has ceased.

I do not feel sorry for the late marquess. One may only guess at how many he has killed over the centuries. More, he is a self-admitted regicide, and my ancient York-

ist ancestors seem to be calling out from the time of Bosworth that, at long last, one of the Lancastrian murderers
has finally been brought to justice. It will do nothing for
poor King Richard, to be sure, whatever may have become
of his body, but, perhaps, it will provide some measure of
solace for his tormented soul.

As I wrote up my notes for Ralph Wattley's gout, I gazed
across the room, once more reminded that Sir Ulrich had
some fancies that were simply wrong. He was right about
the stake, but wrong about beheading. The proof of that
sat quietly in the old chair in the corner of my study, reading Scott's tale of Saxon knights, Templars, true love, and
chivalry in the days of the first King Richard.

I felt no fear at all. True, she had told me that she
would, no doubt, one day bring me into the vampire fold.
When that day comes, I suppose I shall welcome it, for
by then I will no doubt be quite ancient, and near death.
Until then I am safe, if safe is truly the correct word.

Poor, dear Naomi, we have so ill-treated her in our
quest to save Lady Anna. Ravensbrook was the villain, not
she. Her sole victim was more accident than intentional.
Raised from the dead, emerging from her grave alone,
without her master there to guide her, she simply took
the most convenient victim to obtain the fresh blood she
required to complete her restoration. I might even argue
that I am as much to blame in this as she, for restoring her
body following my post mortem required much more of
those mystical powers through which a vampire lives than
the usual.

Having her head chopped off was evidently less of a
problem. Complete healing required a fair quantity of
blood, but, mindful of what had happened before, this
time a sheep sufficed. As she tried to tell us, before we

forced her hand in the churchyard, whilst she unquestionably needs blood to live, it need not be human.

'Are you content here?' I asked.

Naomi lifted her head from her book and nodded. 'I had always hoped I might find myself living in your house one day,' she replied. 'These are not exactly the circumstances I imagined, but I am content.'

'I have seen you angry,' I said. 'I should not wish to see that again. You were — rather terrifying in your fury.'

She placed the open book pages-down on the table in front of the lamp and rose from her chair. She walked across the room, bent over my chair, and placed a tender kiss on my forehead. 'Oh, my poor darling,' she sighed. 'That was not a good night to be re-introduced. And I do not think that that was fury. No, dear, I would say it was frustration, if anything. All I wanted was for you and your friends to understand.

'And, today, you have freed me. Lord Ravensbrook is truly dead. Even tucked safely in my coffin, behind a heavy locked strong room door in your cellar, resting the dreamless rest of my kind, I could feel the weight lifting from my soul. With the master dead, I am truly my own woman once again. So long as he held power over me, there was a compulsion to drink from the throats of living men and women. With him gone, so is that need. The abattoir will supply all my needs from this time forward.'

She sat on my lap, resting one slender arm across my shoulders. Her soft lips pressed against mine. I had never known such contentment.

XLI: Lady Anna Corwin's Journal

Saturday, 3rd August— I woke this morning with dear Suzanne's arm thrown across my torso, her sweet face pressed against my shoulder, her sleeping breath moving a few stray hairs that fell across her face. I do not know how long I simply lay like that, gazing upon my dearest friend, now once more returned to my bed.

For the first time in what seemed like forever, I slept through the night without the disturbance of strange, sexual dreams of our now-late neighbour interrupting my slumber. Why do I call them dreams? I know now that they were quite real, a violation not only of my psyche, but of my body as well. That is the strange power of the vampire at work. What repels also attracts, and the attraction is far, far stronger than the repulsion. It is like the poor wretch who spends his life in an opium den, though he wants nothing more than to return to his loving family, he is unable to overcome the power of the insidious resin in his pipe.

So it was with me. I wanted to follow all of Sir Ulrich's instructions. I knew that I was safer if I wore the garlic garland—and thank Heaven Lord Ravensbrook is now truly dead, and I can safely banish the noisome herbs from my presence—yet at a mere mental command I would throw it off to give my oppressor access to me.

Did poor Naomi Cooper act in the same way? Was she both repelled and enticed, as I was? Sadly, we shall never know, for she was not saved from the monster before death came to her, and now she is truly dead, her pitiful body mouldering in the unused niche in our old family vault in the churchyard.

I have read my brother's journal for the time since Suzanne first arrived. I read it with some degree of annoyance, to be sure, for even as I have the good sense to keep mine in a private cipher, he writes his out in plain English, any need for secrecy protected only by his admittedly horrible penmanship. It might almost be a cipher, though I can read it easily enough, and, I think, anyone else could manage with some difficulty. What they did to the poor girl strikes me as tragic. What he describes the three of us doing in his studio would have been better left unrecorded, no matter how much we all enjoyed the experience.

Suzanne began to stir, opening her eyes to find me smiling at her.

'Did you sleep well?' she asked.

I nodded my head. 'Very well,' I replied. 'Better, now that you are back here.'

Her hand moved down from my shoulder, the open palm coming to rest on my left breast, cupping it through the thin cotton material of my night dress. Impulsively, I leaned my head over and kissed her soft lips.

'I wish I could stay with you forever,' she said. 'I wish that we could flaunt convention, say "to hell with society," and remain together, like this, always.'

'I have been thinking about that,' I replied. 'There might be a way.'

'Do you think so?'

'I have two suitors now, but I care for neither of them, and they will certainly be disappointed in their quest.' I smiled. 'I think they are only after our money, in any case.'

Suzanne looked at me sceptically. 'I thought you didn't really have any money.'

'Not as much as people think,' I said, 'but we are not exactly poor, either. In any event, what I was thinking, a young gentlewoman should not go about on her own. You do not come from a noble background, it is true, but your father was of the professional class, and you might even be called an heiress, with your annuity and the expectation of property to come. You could stay on here, as my companion.'

'Is that practical, dear?' Suzanne asked. 'What would Maureen—that is, O'Leary—have to say about that? Would she not be jealous?'

'Dear Maureen is a servant,' I explained, 'and she knows exactly where she fits into the hierarchy of this household. You are, if not noble, certainly a gentlewoman, and a companion is, after all, not a servant, but a family member. You would continue to take your meals with us, there would be a small salary, which you might easily put aside, as you would incur few actual expenses here, and the room across from mine would become yours.'

'You're banishing me across the corridor again?' Suzanne asked, her tone light and mildly mocking.

'Only your wardrobe,' I laughed. 'I would certainly prefer if you continued to sleep in here with me. Two women cannot marry, but they may certainly enjoy each other's company in the most intimate ways, so long as they are discrete.'

Suzanne kissed me with unconcealed passion. 'I must say,' she told me, when our lips were apart at last, 'that your offer certainly seems better than taking a position as a governess, which had seemed my most likely fate. And, if we cannot officially marry, we can still behave as if we were in private. So, yes, of course, if you create the position, I will certainly accept it.'

I sat up in bed and pulled my night dress off over my head. 'We should celebrate that,' I said.

Suzanne laughed and quickly removed her night dress. My eyes were drawn to the flaming nest of bright red hair between her slender legs. I pushed her back onto the bed and bent over her, kissing her breasts, leaving a trail of kisses down her body, through the short, kinky hairs, and onto her sweet quim. I could feel her hands on my legs, pulling me above her, so that she could pull down on my arse whilst raising her head and get her tongue working between my nether lips.

My body thrilled to the sensual spasms, pure waves of pleasure running right through me as climax followed upon climax. Sweet, musky gushes of feminine passion welled up from Suzanne's heated centre, and I lapped it up, as eagerly as a kitten is drawn to a bowl of milk.

I do not know how long we made love. One hour? Two? Longer? We are so well-suited to each other that, when we make love, it is as if there is only a single being there, our passions merged and united, joining us together in a bond of intimate pleasurings as deep and meaningful as any couple who once stood before a vicar and merged their lives.

And now, I shall have her for as long as I wish. I do not believe either of us shall ever marry, unless the day comes when we could marry each other. I do not imagine that day will ever come, however, so we shall simply have to make do.

XLII: Doctor Allen's Journal

Monday, 23rd September— I opened my new practice today. Even a few months ago, had someone suggested I would leave High Coulston and take up a practice in Birmingham, I would have called him a fool. Yet, here I am, moved away from all of my old patients and friends.

I do not regret it. As I write this, Naomi is resting in a strong room some thoughtful prior owner had built in the cellar. Directly we moved in, I installed a comfortable bed in that room. It is pure myth that a vampire must sleep in a coffin. Naomi sleeps in a bed, with a sheet and blanket drawn over her lithe form. It is true, once she falls into her un-dead slumber, she sleeps with the same utter stillness of a corpse, but still, she sleeps in a bed. Locked away in the cellar, where no light ever penetrates, she is as safe as she can ever be in a world were most men do not even believe vampires exist, but those men who do can be deadly.

She has been true to her word. Though she must drink blood to survive, she obtains it from dumb animals, not from men. Indeed, she has vowed to me that she will not drink the blood of any human being ever again, unless, when I am old, it becomes my wish to remain with her forever and become a vampire in my turn. Still, if she has proven an essentially harmless vampire, her face was too familiar around High Coulston for us to safely remain there.

In Birmingham, no one knows her. No one knows either of us, except for Nigel Ralston, an old friend from my days at university. But Nigel knows nothing about Naomi, other than that she is with me, that we are married—or so we now tell the world—and that we appear to love each other very much. He simply accepts her as a quite ordinary woman with a poor appetite. He has no need to know that, very often, the 'red wine' in her glass once flowed through the veins of a steer.

I feel we are safe here.

But, now I hear the cellar door opening, and soft footfalls upon the wooden floor of the kitchen hall. I shall put this journal aside, for my love is with me again.